# THE L

**Bianca Bellová** was born in Prague and grew-up as the communist regime of Czechoslovakia began to fracture. This background provided the material for her first book, *Sentimental Novel.* She has since written four further novels and worked as both a translator and interpreter.

*The Lake* won the Czech nationals Magnesia Litera Book of the Year Award and European Prize for Literature in 2017. It has been translated into over twenty languages.

# THE LAKE

Bianca Bellová

Translated from the Czech by
Alex Zucker

PARTHIAN

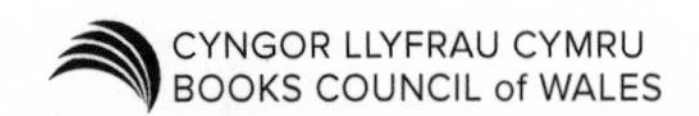

Co-funded by the Creative Europe Programme of
the European Union

This translation was made possible by a grant
from the Ministry of Culture of the Czech Republic

**Alex Zucker** has translated novels by the Czech authors Bianca Bellová, Petra Hůlová, Jáchym Topol, J. R. Pick, Magdaléna Platzová, Tomáš Zmeškal, Josef Jedlička, Heda Margolius Kovály, Patrik Ouředník, and Miloslava Holubová. He has also Englished stories, plays, subtitles, young adult and children's books, song lyrics, reportages, essays, poems, philosophy, art history, and an opera. His translation of Petra Hůlová's *Three Plastic Rooms* and Jáchym Topol's *The Devil's Workshop* received Writing in Translation awards from English PEN, and in 2010 he won the National Translation Award from the American Literary Translators Association for his translation of Petra Hůlová's debut novel, *All This Belongs to Me*. Alex is a past cochair of the Translation Committee at PEN America, and his collaboration with the Authors Guild has thus far resulted in the first national survey of working conditions for literary translators in the U.S., the creation of a Translators Group within the Guild, and the Guild's first model contract for literary translation. More at alexjzucker.com.

Parthian, Cardigan SA43 1ED
www.parthianbooks.com
First Published as *Jezero*

ISBN print: 978-1-913640-52-1
ISBN ebook: 978-1-913640-90-3
Editor: Gina Rathbone
Cover Design: Syncopated Pandemonium
Typeset by Elaine Sharples
Printed by 4edge Limited
Published with the financial support of the Books Council of Wales and the Ministry of Culture of the Czech Republic
Co-funded by the Creative Europe Programme of the European Union
The publishers would like to thank Edgar de Bruin of Agency Pluh, Amsterdam in making this project possible.
British Library Cataloguing in Publication Data
A cataloguing record for this book is available from the British Library.

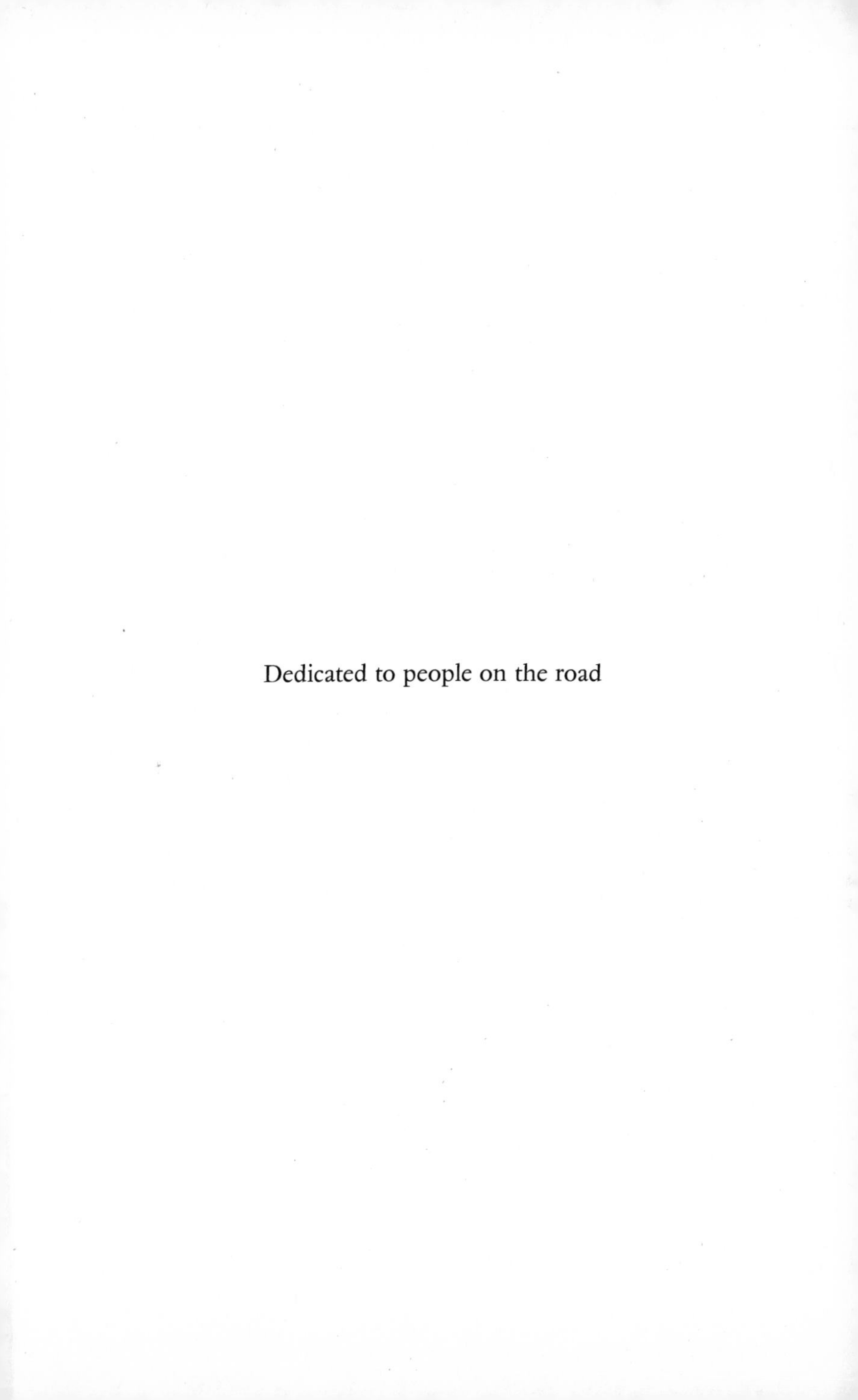

Dedicated to people on the road

# I
# Embryo

Nami, bathed in sweat, holds his gramma's blubbery hand. The waves from the lake slap against the concrete pier. He hears screams, more like shrieks, coming from the town beach. If he's on the blanket with his gramma and grampa, it must be a Sunday. There's one other person there too. Nami pictures three dark spots, the three triangles of a bikini, with a long dark tail of hair hanging down, brushed out like the tail of a horse, and two dark tufts of hair visible in the underarms. The three triangles move slowly in the sun, turning over again and again, until there's only one. A little way offshore, a catfish lazily flicks its tail.

'The surface seems lower than it used to be,' Nami's gramma says, smacking a fly as it lands on her belly. She chews roasted sunflower seeds, purchased from the stand on the beach, spitting the shells onto the concrete in front of her.

'What're you talking about?' Nami's grampa laughs. 'Women's wisdom–second worst thing in the world, next to a hangover!'

He rocks back and forth as he laughs, hands on his thighs. In one hand, wedged between the dirty, chewed-up fingers, is an unfiltered cigarette.

The three triangles pick up a thermos, turn to Nami, and pour him a cup of mint tea.

'Have a drink, dove.' Well, what do you know? The three triangles have a voice. It's pleasantly deep, like the old well behind their house. Nami takes a drink. The honey-sweetened tea is delicious, sliding easily down his throat.

'Let's go, dove,' his grampa says. 'You don't want anyone calling you a sissy. Every boy around here can swim by the time they're three.'

He runs a hand over his rounded belly. Flicks the cigarette butt into the water, where it lands with a hiss. Nami doesn't want to go in the water. He wants to lie on the blanket, resting his head on his gramma's soft belly and watching the three red triangles. He attempts to lift a hand, but it just drops lazily back in his lap.

'Go on, Nami,' his gramma says. 'I'll buy you a lollipop.'

The cellophane always sticks to the lollipop. You can never get it off. The only time Nami ever gets one is on World Peace Day or when the three triangles come to visit. He doesn't really like the taste of burnt sugar and violets, but he so rarely gets one that he always looks forward to it and is willing to do whatever he's asked.

Nami slowly gets to his feet, but before he can fully stand he finds himself flying through the air.

'Now swim, sturgeon!' his grampa shouts, bursting into laughter. The three triangles scream. So does Nami's gramma. Landing painfully on his side, Nami breaks through the surface and sinks down into the dark water. Looking up, he can see the faint shine of the sun in the swarm of bubbles trailing behind him.

His lungs ache, he's had the wind knocked out of him. The deeper he sinks, the colder the water gets. Nami sinks numbly, arms outstretched, flapping at his side. Any second now, he thinks, he's going to see the Lake Spirit. The pressure on his lungs grows, his ears feel like they're about to explode. Instinctively he gasps for breath and swallows a mouthful of water. He can't see anymore. Waving his arms and legs wildly, he makes his way toward the surface. Everything is black and shiny.

'Stupid old fool,' his gramma says as Nami finally catches

his breath, furiously coughing up dirty water. 'You old ass, I wouldn't trust you with a can of worms!'

'What's wrong? He's fine, isn't he? You saw the boy swim, right?' Nami's grampa says in a defensive tone. His voice is trembling slightly. 'A true warrior!'

'Come here, dove,' the three triangles say from the depths of the earth, wrapping Nami in their arms. One pounding chest on another. Nami settles down and stops coughing. The skin beneath the triangles is warm and bronze and smells nice. The three triangles hold him close, kissing his hair and speaking in whispers. The woman's hair tickles his face, and she begins to sing.

'Stop singing to him!' Nami's gramma shouts. Nami shudders, then lies still, not moving a muscle. He pretends that he's dead, that he's not even there. The singing falls away to nothing but a thick sound with each exhale, like a bell's vibrations dying down after the clapper has stopped. Nami wishes he could stay that way forever. He steals a glance at the woman's face, but all he can see is the tip of her nose and her prominent cheekbones. As they're walking home, Nami faints and his grampa has to carry him.

Instead of passing through the square with the statue of the Statesman and the ditch the Russians bulldozed for people to dump trash in, they take the back way, around the apartment complex.

'You're quite a load, boy,' grumbles Nami's grampa. His foot slips and he stiffens, barely catching his balance in time to avoid a fall. When they reach home, Nami gets his lollipop. He licks it more out of obligation than enjoyment while furtively keeping his eye on the three triangles, which meanwhile have changed into a blue-and-green flower-print dress. As soon as he has the chance, he reaches out to touch it, and is rewarded with a wonderful smell.

That evening Nami has a violent fit of nausea. His

stomach contracts uncontrollably, ejecting torrents of dirty water, mint tea, and lumps of sheep cheese blini. The blue-and-green flower-print dress strokes his forehead, holding his head while he vomits, wiping his mouth and whispering in a soothing voice. 'Shh, dove, everything's going to be all right.'

The next morning when Nami wakes up, the blue-and-green dress is gone. He takes a sip of black Russian tea and throws it back up immediately.

***

Nami grew up surrounded by the smell of fish, so he never really noticed it. The small town of Boros has a sturgeon hatchery and, right next door, a fish processing plant. Alea, their neighbour, works in the fish factory. Sometimes she comes over to sit on their stoop and brings a bucket of caviar to trade for a sack of potatoes. Then Nami eats caviar every day for breakfast and dinner. He sits over the bucket, scooping it up by the spoonful until he's sick to his stomach.

'You ate it all?' asks his gramma.

Nami lowers his eyes and stares at the floor.

'That's all right,' she says. 'Caviar is the healthiest thing in the world. After ginseng!'

'And after a good fuck,' says the old man with a grin from the corner of the room. He rubs the corner of his eye with his thumb, gripping an unfiltered cigarette between his index finger and his misshapen middle finger.

'Grampa, you should be ashamed!' Nami's gramma chides him. But she's grinning too. She fries a batch of blini and slathers them with butter. 'You eat like a VIP,' she says, smiling at Nami as she fills his plate. Nami likes caviar, but he feels like that can't be all there is. He hopes that something more meaningful lies in store, but at four years old he doesn't have the words yet to express it. He crushes the little black beads between his teeth, absently picking at the scab on his knee.

His gramma has a big lump on her tailbone, broad bony hips, and a soft tummy Nami likes to fall asleep on. She strokes his hair with a hard, dry hand as she tells him stories about the Spirit of the Lake and the warriors of the Golden Horde, who sleep in Kolos Mountain, waiting until the great warrior comes to wake them up.

'Will that be me?' Nami asks.

'Of course it will, my boy,' his gramma smiles.

'But how will I find them?'

'Providence will show you the way, dove.' Nami hears his gramma's words and peacefully drifts off to sleep.

***

It's Fishery Day, the biggest holiday of the year. The whole town gathers on the square around the statue of the Statesman, the children dressed in snow-white shirts, boys with colourful neckties, girls with bows in their hair. Akel the vendor, who normally sells herring and sunflower seeds from his stall, also has cotton candy and luscious doughnuts, soaked in burned fat. Today is the day when none of the fishermen go out on the lake because they're all celebrating. By eleven a.m., almost nobody is left standing on their feet; they have sacrificed too mightily to the Spirit of the Lake.

The chairman of the fish processing plant gives a long speech, singing the praises of progress and collectivization as he shifts his gaze from the lake to the sky and back again. A man with a shaman's headdress on–though nobody mentions him, as if he weren't really there–dances around the statue of the Statesman. The Russian engineers and their wives, standing in the first line of listeners, are dressed in big-city fashion; the women in high heels, leather purses over their arms, hair brushed high. The local women speak of them with contempt; sometimes they even spit. One of the small Russian boys, despite the dumb look on his face, is an object of admiration, riding back and forth across the square in a squeaky pedal car. Nami can't take his eyes off him. He grips his gramma's sweaty hand, crossing his legs; he badly needs to go pee. In one hand he holds a parade waver shaped like a fish. His grampa stands next to him on the other side, swaying unsteadily, head drooping; every now and then he loudly smacks his lips. They hear the sound of thunder, or maybe gunfire from the Russian barracks. The Russian engineers and their wives look at one another in disgust and shake their heads. Nobody has been listening to the speech for a while now. The women converse in a lowered voice, but no one leaves, out of courtesy. They all have their minds on the banquet that awaits them in the fish processing plant: blini with caviar, herring in mayonnaise, onion tarts, blackberry wine for the women, and plenty of hard liquor for their men. Nami can't stop watching the green pedal car, cruising over the bumps and potholes like a tank. He tries to look away but can't. Even when he shuts his eyes, he still sees the car. His insides ache, squirming with envy.

'Can we go now, Gramma?'

'Soon, just hold on.'

'How much longer?'

'Just a little while.'

For a five-year-old boy, a little while is practically an eternity.

'Gramma?'

'What is it now?'

Nami doesn't say a word.

'You peed yourself.'

Nami's grampa wakes from his snooze and glances around uncertainly.

'The boy peed himself,' Nami's gramma whispers, elbowing the old man.

'Idiot,' he rasps.

A stain slowly spreads across the front of Nami's shorts as a stream of urine runs down his thighs. It thunders again, this time with lightning too. Wind whips the last few pages of the speech the factory chairman still has left in front of him, and without further warning the sky rips open, gushing water like when Nami's gramma empties out the washtub. As the women's hair collapses, blue make-up streams down their faces in hydrologic maps, their high heels slipping in the mud that has suddenly formed on the square, but the chairman of the fish factory goes on speaking. The statue of the Statesman silently raises its arms to the sky. Nami is instantly soaked to the skin. All that's left of his parade wand is a wooden rod and streaks of red paint on his arm. The square has turned into a ploughed field, people sunk in mud up to their ankles and losing their shoes. The boy in the pedal car gets stuck in the mud and starts to cry. Nami's grampa tips back his head and lets the rain fall on his face. The square lies on a slight slope, so it doesn't take the boys long to realise the mud is great for sliding in. Akel desperately tries to keep his stand from slipping away downhill. Doughnuts tumble off the counter, dropping in the mud.

'It's the Apocalypse,' Nami's grampa mumbles, beginning to sober up.

Water continues to pour from the sky, gradually filling the boy's pedal car. The microphone gives out entirely, but the chairman goes on speaking. It's like a silent comedy, except for the roar of the rain and the thunder, which every now and then strikes so close by that Nami's gramma twitches and looks toward the lake in terror. The shaman slowly walks away, gripping his headdress. Then, following his lead, the crowd hypnotically stirs into motion. The factory chairman lowers his arm holding the microphone. Water runs down the collar of his jacket, down his shirt. He gazes accusingly at the sky. Nami can't help himself, overcome by uncontrollable laughter, giggling like a madman. His gramma rolls her eyes at him, but Nami just laughs even more, still laughing hysterically as his gramma drags him home by the hand.

Nami doesn't stop laughing until they cross the threshold of his house. His gramma slaps him across his sopping-wet thighs and his laughter finally stops, but he still hiccups long into the night.

They caught a lot of fish that year.

***

Sometimes Nami wakes up in bed in the morning with the sun shining into his eyes. It must be vacation, or his gramma would have woken him up. It's probably warmer outside than indoors. From the kitchen Nami can hear his grampa's smoker's cough and the horn of a tugboat in the distance. He throws his arms and legs wide on the bed and stares up at the ceiling, where bunches of thyme and lady's mantle are drying. He feels like he could spend the rest of his life like this. If he sits up in bed, he can see all the way to the lake. He stretches out and puts on his clothes. On the kitchen table he finds a plateful of doughnuts waiting, fried for breakfast by his gramma. They're only lukewarm now. He runs outside, determined to build a hideout in the branches that will last—not like last time, when the whole thing fell apart and he got a scrape on his back.

The only tree for miles around is a cherry tree with a

reddish-brown trunk that got struck by lightning, now half its branches are withered. Nami drags over a few large boards of various length and thickness. As they slip and start to fall, he has to tie them together with rope. He tries to nail them in place with his grampa's carpenter's hammer, which weighs at least ten pounds. The tree groans, the branches shake, and the boards resist, sliding away. The nail runs clear through the board into empty space.

'Fucking hell!' Nami screams, throwing the hammer to the ground.

'What are you doing up there, boy?' Nami's grampa bellows, stepping out of the outhouse. 'Lucky for you you don't have a father, you miserable brat, or he'd tan your hide!'

Nami stops and thinks a minute, wondering what it would be like to have his hide tanned by a father. He actually likes the idea.

'Our only tree and he goes and wrecks it. As if he hasn't done enough damage already,' Nami's grampa hollers in the direction of his gramma. She stands with one hand propped on her hip, the other one shading her eyes as she searches for Nami.

Nami sits on the ground now, behind the toolshed, breaking rocks. He lifts the heavy hammer high over his head, then brings it down, closing his eyes. He repeats the motion again and again, till streams of sweat run off him and the stone turns to dust. He finds it satisfying. He stares in amazement at the palms of his hands, which have broken out in huge blisters.

He tosses the hammer into the grass and runs down to the lake to wash off the dust.

'C'mere, you little runt! I'll hammer you like a nail!' his grampa shouts after him.

Nami keeps running. He knows his grampa will never catch him.

***

'I don't know, but it seems weird to me, having the fish processing plant right next to the hatchery,' Nami's neighbour Alea muses. 'I know fish've got little brains, but still. It's like putting a graveyard next to the hospital where babies are born, don't you think?'

'Pour us some more chardonnay, boy,' Nami's gramma says, sitting at the table. Nami tops up their shot glasses with potato spirits. His gramma runs a hand over the plastic tablecloth, breathes a sigh, and stares off into the distance.

'Not a lot of em either and they're dyin like flies,' Alea goes on. 'What?' Nami's gramma replies absently. Today she and Alea are rolling dough for bureks, one sheet after the next, coating it with a layer of butter, then laying another layer on top. Instead of a rolling pin, they use a three-foot-long wooden bar, like the one they have in the school gymnasium.

Nami's gramma huffs and puffs, setting her hands behind her hips and stretching her back.

'The sturgeons,' Alea says, visibly annoyed.

The house is painted blue, with a white roof. The door is made of hard black locust. The roof has a hole in it. When the weather's nice, it lets in sunbeams; when it's raining, water. Little snakes live underneath the old floorboards, but they're harmless, vanishing into the cracks at the first sound of footsteps. Nami's gramma says they keep good luck in the house, and pours milk into a dish for them.

The house sits on a little hill, with a view overlooking the lake. From the front door you can see the boats sailing back into port. There's just a single step up to the stoop with the railing. Nami's gramma likes to sit there and watch the men return home. Elbows propped against the table, she knits, embroiders, slices vegetables for dinner, peels potatoes, pits cherries with a hairpin, receives visitors.

'I don't like the look of it,' she says wearily. Heavy clouds are gathering on the horizon, where the lake comes to an end. That usually means a storm on the way.

'Don't be so gloomy!' says Alea. 'More chardonnay, Nami. We get those clouds from the east here every April.' The old lady sighs, sprinkling lumps of sheep cheese onto the layer of dough.

'Look, the Spirit is frowning. He's still angry.'

'Be quiet.'

'That wasn't enough.'

'Shush!'

'He still wants more!'

The sky above the lake looks heavy as lead. The ponderous clouds cover over the horizon like a fat old man atop his wife on their wedding night. Nami gathers snails from the garden and stacks them in a pile. He calls it snail school, pairing them up on benches and frowning as he scolds them for giving the wrong answer. Sometimes he even uses a cane.

'I'm worried, Alea,' Nami's gramma says softly, hanging her hands at her side. 'Me too, you old goose,' Alea says, giving her a hug. Hanging on each other, the two women form a sculpture, squeezing each other as hard as they can, trembling–how many times have they done this before?

Someday, someone will make a statue of the fisherman's wife, shading her eyes as she gazes out to the horizon; whole throngs of women, their right arms taut with muscle from constantly gazing out to sea.

'Go fetch the shaman, Nami!' his gramma calls to him.

'You're not going anywhere, Nami,' Alea says. 'Your gramma's drunk.'

Nami rubs his hands on his thighs, awaiting further orders.

'They'll come back like they always do, silly. Don't get

hysterical,' Alea says, patting Nami's gramma awkwardly on the wrist.

As Nami's gramma pulls the burek out of the oven, the first drops begin to fall. The two women chew the buttery dough in silence, peering out the window through the torrents of pouring rain.

Upstairs, Nami lies on the floor in his room, drawing in a notepad with his grampa's purple-ink pen. The rain pounds the windowpanes as the sheet covering the shed flaps loose in the wind. Nami has the transistor radio on, tuned to the same program he listens to every evening. A soothing female voice recites the twenty-four-hour weather forecast for sailors and fishermen. In a rich, full alto, she recites the wind speed and expected rainfall and cloud conditions for each individual part of the lake. She announces gale-force winds of 10 on the Beaufort scale with the same steady voice as she does a breeze rustling the leaves in the trees. Nami finds it calming. He lays his head down on the floor and goes to sleep. When he wakes up in the morning, the sky looks swept clean and the sun is blazing hot. His body feels like it's broken and he's starving. As he goes downstairs to get breakfast, he looks at his hands and discovers they're covered in purple ink. There's a candle burning on the kitchen table, and his gramma sits in the corner, leaning her back against the wall, staring wide-eyed straight ahead. Nami's grampa, Alea's husband, and six other fishermen are missing.

***

Nami sits on the pavement at the bus stop, feet protruding into the roadway.

'What're you doin?' Alex asks. Alex is Alea's son. His father died out on the lake along with Nami's grampa. Alex is red-haired and freckled, just like his mother.

'Shootin Russkies,' Nami answers calmly, wiping his nose on his sleeve.

A Russian jeep drives past, stirring up dust in its wake. A Russian man, smoking, frowns behind the wheel. As he passes, Nami hefts an imaginary machine gun, narrows one eye, and sprays the jeep with bullets, from right to left, then back again.

'You wasted him.' Alex nods approvingly and sits down next to Nami. 'Clean job!'

There isn't much work to do. The road is oversized and traffic is light, apart from Peace Day and Fishery Day. Occasionally a truck passes by on its way to the fish processing plant, or a piece of heavy equipment headed for the port. A few Russian jeeps, a bus a couple of times a day. A flock of sheep walking east in the morning, then back in the afternoon.

The two of them work together now, Nami firing the machine gun, Alex throwing hand grenades. Crouching down before each explosion, they triumphantly high five when the result is spectacular, with bits of gear and human bodies flying through the air. Nami spits with satisfaction. The ball of phlegm hits the ground and rolls, gathering dust till it comes to a stop at a pair of red tennis shoes.

'Keep shooting Russian cars and not only will you get your asses kicked, but they'll put your parents against the wall,' says the head above the sneakers. It belongs to a girl from that new girls' school on the square. She is probably about the same age as them–nine or ten–and has a big yellow bow in her hair.

'I don't have any parents,' says Nami, narrowing his eyes.

The girl stares a moment, then shrugs and walks away.

'I'd fuck her,' says Alex, giving an approving nod.

'You'd fuck your own gramma,' says Nami, spitting into the dust again.

They watch a half-loaded container ship as it sails out of port.

'I was up all night puking,' says Alex in a jaded voice.

'Did you swim in the lake?' Nami asks.

'Yeah, all morning.'

'I always puke after I swim.'

The girl with the bow is no longer in sight. The sky rumbles, and a moment later three fighter planes pass overhead. The boys take aim with their virtual weapons and gun the jets down from the sky. Then spit approvingly in the dust.

***

On the hill above the port, on either side of the dirt road, are the fishermen's houses; at the end of the road is a stand selling herring and another with sunflower seeds. In summer, the guy with the cotton candy comes and rents out the former pub at the end of the street. The homes are solid, brick, mostly one-storey; only a few—including the one where Nami and his gramma live—have a second floor. Fishermen's Lane, they call it, and it's the town's unofficial heart.

West of Fishermen's Lane are the institutional buildings—outpatient clinic, house of culture, post office, school—and the homes of the other inhabitants, erected with no apparent plan. Little of the town is arranged into streets, with buildings cropping up in random and often surprising formations. On the east side is the housing estate for Russian engineers, with the notable square and the statue of the Statesman. Still further to the east lies the woods, which has had to be partially cut back due to construction, and then the barracks.

You can hear the accordion music and drunken shouts all the way from the housing estate. Built for the Russians, the housing estate consists of a few prefab apartment blocks arranged at right angles, with built-in vodka cabinets in every flat—or at least that's the rumour—a shopping centre with a cinema, and a hotel with a swimming pool. A swimming pool! The statue of the Statesman looms over the concrete square. Enormous bras and bloomers of indeterminate colour hang side by side with colourful linens, drying on lines strung crookedly from metal poles embedded in concrete amid the prefab blocks. The uniforms on the line flutter in the wind, from time to time pausing mid-flight to respectfully salute the statue of the Statesman.

'The Russians're celebrating. We're in for another whoop-de-do night,' Nami's gramma sighs, rubbing camel fat into her cracked heels. 'I just hope they won't start shooting again.'

'They won't,' Nami says. 'Those are the engineers in the housing estate, not the meatheads from the barracks.'

'Same difference. Pour me some chardonnay, dove.'

'Gramma?'

'Yeah?'

'My bones hurt, especially at night. It keeps waking me up.'

'Which ones, dove?'

Nami runs his hands over his shins. 'Here.'

'Have you been getting up to no good? Under the blanket? Have you? Because if you have, the pain is a punishment.'

'Come on, Gramma.'

'I'm just asking.'

'Gramma, that's embarrassing.'

'Embarrassing or not, I won't have you getting up to no good as long as you're under my roof. Take the comfrey salve down from the shelf and rub some of that on.'

Nami gets up and pours his gramma a shot. Then searches through the jars on the shelf.

'This one?'

'That's axle grease, you dodo. Next to it, over there ... in the purple box maybe ... try that.'

'It stinks like a sore foot.'

'That's the one.'

Nami spreads the foul-smelling substance over his shins and slowly rubs it in.

'So you know for sure this'll help?'

'You're as cheeky as your grandad, dove.' Nami's gramma nods, then pauses for a moment. 'Nobody ever tells you how sad you'll be without them,' she says with a dramatic sigh.

Nami frowns. The smell of the ointment is numbing. 'He was always being rude to you. He beat you constantly. Last time he knocked your tooth out, remember?'

She waves dismissively. 'If he walked in that door right now, I'd offer my face and ask for one more.'

Nami shakes his head but keeps his thoughts to himself, noticing his gramma softly crying and wiping the tears from her face with her dirty fingers.

'There's nothing worse than being by yourself,' she sobs. Nami's gramma often gets emotional, and enjoys it, so Nami takes it in his stride. Besides, being by himself is his favourite thing in the world.

'Poor thing. At least he's in the lake and not lying out in the desert somewhere.'

'Gramma, where're my parents? How come I don't have a father and mother like everyone else?'

His gramma doesn't hear.

'Gramma! Where is that lady who came to the lake with us that time when Grampa threw me in and he was trying to teach me to swim? She had a red swimsuit and she held my head when I threw up.'

His gramma defiantly tosses her head, the same way

Nami sometimes did when the teacher asked why he didn't have his homework. Then studies the backs of her hands, speckled with tiny blooms of eczema.

'Sounds like a dream to me. But maybe our neighbour Alea. She sometimes used to come swimming with us.'

'No.' Nami shook his head. 'Alea's fat and redheaded and stinks of fish.'

'Time to go to bed,' Nami's gramma says. 'You need to get to sleep so you won't miss school tomorrow. I couldn't even wake you this morning.'

Nami sighs and gets to his feet. Bends over and rolls his pants back down over his shins. His gramma can see they're too short–they barely come to his ankles–but doesn't say anything.

'And wash your mouth out with soap, you impudent loudmouth,' she calls after him.

***

He sees the girl with the yellow bow on his way home from school almost every day, although sometimes the bow is blue or polka-dot. They both lower their eyes as they pass to avoid looking at each other. Nami's throat clenches up a little every time.

'I'd bet my boots she's a good fuck,' says Alex. Nami as usual ignores him. He buys a bag of roasted sunflower seeds from Akel's stand and sits down on the pavement at the bus stop, spitting the shells onto the road.

'Hey, studs,' two older boys walking by call out to them. They go to a higher grade in the same school and already shave. All of the mothers and fathers in Boros want their boys to do well in school and attend the naval academy, but most of them are dimwits and end up on fishing boats just like their fathers.

'Hey, studs, you up for a fuck?' one of the older boys asks, flicking a cigarette butt across the street in a well-practiced arc.

'Depends,' Alex says in a guarded tone, blinking nervously.

'How bout you,' says the jerk, giving Nami a kick in the foot. 'I bet you've never even fucked, have you?'

'Course I have. I fucked your mother.'

The other jerk laughs.

'All right then. If you want to miss out on the fuck of your life ...' the first jerk says in an irritated voice. His whole face is just one giant zit.

A dry afternoon wind blows off the desert as they make their way through the little town. The camels bray. The sun is hot and their foreheads are covered in sweat. They walk through the Russian housing estate, past the fish processing plant, the dry docks, and then head uphill into the gypsy quarter. The area is deserted, except for an old gypsy woman smoking a pipe with a scarf on her head in front of a wooden shack.

'Gypsy girls, huh?' Alex whispers knowingly. Nami moseys along in the back, hands shoved in his pockets. The jerks grin eagerly, exchanging winks.

'That's it there,' says Acne Boy, pointing to the one brick house on the lane. It has an entry gate, but no fence.

'Hey!' the other jerk shouts. A red-haired dog asleep on the stoop warily raises its head, then jumps to its feet.

'What, are you guarding the place, you hairy fleabag piece of shit?' Acne Boy laughs.

The dog starts ferociously barking, then comes after them.

'Run for it!' Nami shouts, and the four of them go sprinting back down the gypsy lane. The two jerks jump onto a wagon parked in front of a hut, laughing like maniacs, while Nami and Alex keep running, the dog white with rage at their heels. The old gypsy woman calls out after them, but Nami's afraid the dog is going to tear a hole in his pants and his gramma will go out of her mind.

Alex turns to look back and trips.

'Shit on a stick!' he cries.

In an instant, the dog is on top of him, front legs encircling Alex's thigh, humping his back and copulating with Alex's calf.

'Nami! For God's sake, get him off me!' Alex cries. The dog, no longer barking, tongue hanging out, mechanically bangs up and down with a brain-dead look on his face. Nami stops and watches, feeling sorry for his friend. The two jerks are laughing so hard they have tears running down their faces. One of them cracks up so hard he actually falls out of the wagon.

'How's that for a proper fuck? Nice one, right?' he shouts, bursting into giggles.

The dog finishes its business and trots off a few steps, standing there staring at Alex with the same brain-dead expression still, tongue out, panting fast. Nami throws a stone at the dog, who lets out a bark of pain and surprise and runs away. Alex gets up and walks to the other side of the lane, dragging his mated leg behind him as if it didn't belong to him.

***

Sometimes the two jerks lay in wait for Nami on his way to school. They're a head taller than he is, but Nami is faster. Usually he outruns them. When they do manage to catch him, though, one of the boys holds him tight while the other one gropes his crotch. Then they let him go with a kick or two, just for good measure.

'Faggots!' Nami calls after them, dusting off his pants. 'Dog fuckers!'

The day Nami discovers the first whisker on his face in the mirror, he determinedly shaves it off with his grampa's razor and cuts himself. Now running late for school, he has no choice but to pass through the housing estate, where the two jerks are waiting. They stand, legs spread, in the middle of the dusty road, hands in their pockets, wearing tough looks. The school is in sight, but too far away.

'Fuck off, faggots. I'm in a rush!' Nami cries. He speeds up and tries to run between them, but Acne Boy sticks out his leg and Nami goes sailing through the air, landing on his forearms and painfully scraping them. Before he can get up, Acne Boy sits on his back.

'Get off, fuckwad. I'll be late for school.'

The older boy lies on top of him, excitedly whispering in his ear. Nami can feel his warm breath on the back of his neck.

'Get off me, faggot. Your breath stinks. I think I'm gonna puke.'

'Come to the nonstop tonight, baby boy, and we'll try to guess which one of the regulars is your dad.'

'Piss off.'

'Your mother fucked them all.'

'I don't have a mother, moron.'

'What?'

Acne Boy is so confused he loosens his grip on Nami.

'What the fuck're you talkin about?'

Nami slips free and jumps to his feet. But Acne Boy still has his notebooks. He swings the bundle back and forth in front of Nami's face, taunting him.

'I don't have a mother, moron,' Nami repeats with a triumphant smile.

Acne Boy turns to the other jerk in disbelief.

'You hear that? He thinks he doesn't have a mom.'

His jerk friend lets out a braying laugh.

'So how do you think you came into the world, big brain?'

'He probably fell out a camel's ass.'

'Either that or mitosis, from somebody's dick.'

Nami just stands there, unsmiling.

'The moron doesn't know.'

'Nope, he hasn't got a clue.'

'Someone oughta tell him.'

'Faggots.'

'Your mother was such a bitch she let every guy that had a cock stick it in her hole.'

'Retards.'

Nami grabs for his notebooks and Acne Boy relents. It's over. Nami sees the doors close as he walks up to school, but he's no longer in a hurry. He sits down on the stairs in front and scrawls in the dust with a stick. Both his pantlegs are torn at the knee.

***

The nonstop is a concrete hut that looks more like a transformer station, which is what it used to be. A few broken ceramic insulators remain on the wall, clipped wires still sticking out. Only the first three letters light up in the neon sign reading NONSTOP. The door is always open, with strips of rubber hanging from the top to help keep out the flies. Inside, it smells of stale alcohol and moisture-laden tobacco smoke; outside, of hectolitres of excreted urine.

Evenings, when the sun stops beating down on the arid land and sinks behind Kolos Hill, and the wasps are no longer a nuisance, the men emerge from the nonstop with their bottles and cheap tobacco and occupy the plastic tables out in front, with holes burned in them from forgotten cigarettes.

Nami starts to visit the nonstop regularly. He sits on the

ground among the clumps of dry grass, chewing sunflower seeds and spitting the shells into the wind. After a few days the men invite him to join them, and old Karal buys him a shot. Nami drinks it down, then proceeds to entertain the men, slurring his words and reeling around the room, until he trips over a beer crate and falls.

'That's how my camels died,' Karal sighs when he finally stops laughing. He spreads his eczema-disfigured hands wide. 'Just like that: they stuffed their faces with grass, started reelin around, then dropped to the ground and never got up. Took a few days, chokin and bellowin like they were wounded. Had to cut their throats to put an end to it."

Karal falls silent and wipes his eyes.

'Grass is soaked in salt,' says one of the men. 'Makin the livestock sick.'

'Fifty camels, can you imagine?' Karal starts in again. 'Had a dowry for all my daughters. Now I'm bare-assed broke.'

Silence falls over the group. The men look in the direction of where the port used to be and sip liquor from their cups. Glowing dots flare in the dark as the men draw on their cigarettes.

'Fish plant stopped hirin too,' says an old man with one eye.

'Fish plant's been lettin people go for two years now, smarty-pants. Hatchery's likely shuttin down for good.'

'Boy,' one of the men says, turning to Nami. He's still on the ground, looking up at the starry sky swaying unsteadily overhead. 'Hey, boy! Go grab me some herring down at the stand!'

Nami slowly rises up on all fours and vomits. The vomit runs away through the dirt between his hands.

'My camels were pukin just like that!' shouts Karal.

'Whose boy is that?' asks the barkeep, coming outside and leaning against the door frame, folding her arms. She wears a widow's black apron, unruly white hair spilling down around her fleshy face.

'Marina, bring me another bottle,' calls one of the men, but she ignores him.

'Who do you belong to, boy?'

'Hey, boy, bring me some kippers!' one of the men shouts again, then breaks into a cough.

'Fisherman Petr was my grampa,' says Nami, wiping his mouth. A silence descends.

'He's the son of that tart,' says Karal. Nobody says a word still, but a few of the men clear their throats.

'C'mere,' says the barmaid, extending a fat hand to Nami. 'Come inside. Your gramma will be worried. Here, come in, have a seat.' She more or less forces him into a chair inside the nonstop. A dim light shines from behind the bar and a poorly lit portrait of a saint. The music playing softly from the radio makes Nami's stomach lurch again.

The barmaid pours him a glass of water from the tap, sprinkles in a pinch of salt, and stirs.

'Here, drink this. How old are you?'

'Fourteen,' Nami lies.

He takes a sip and spits it back out. 'Yuck, that's disgusting!'

'Just drink it. You'll feel better.'

Nami downs the glass. Despite the utmost revulsion, he manages to keep the contents in his stomach.

'There. Now run along home, dove. Your gramma must be worried.'

'You know my mom?'

The woman stands up straight. The men outside are yelling. The old man with one eye stands in the doorway amid the strips of rubber, asking what's going on.

'I did. Beautiful girl, like she was made of porcelain.'

'What happened to her?'

The woman shrugs.

'You know!'

'Take it easy. I have no idea what happened to her. But she probably went to the city, what else?'

'What city?'

'The capital. That's where everyone goes. Boy, you've got the same brain as your grampa had.'

'I do not!'

'Well, just don't throw up in here.'

Nami starts to gag again. He gingerly gets to his feet, holding onto the table.

'What's her name?'

'Look, ask your gramma.'

Nami frowns.

'God keep you,' she says quietly as he makes to leave. 'Such a strong, healthy, young boy. You should get out of here while you can.'

By the time Nami gets home, all the lights are off. He checks the henhouse door, urinates off the stoop, and slips quietly into the house. His gramma snores loudly, interrupted by long apnoeic pauses.

***

A Russian flotilla rusts in the bay: two battleships, two destroyers, one tanker, a fireboat, and several smaller boats belonging to the coastguard; apart from a single minesweeper, bafflingly perched on its end amid the dry mud, they all lie on their side. The dead fleet no longer holds any interest even for the children in town. They've crawled all over them, inside and out, what's the big deal?

On their annual field trip to the museum, the sixth

graders walk past the wrecks without even noticing; they're as much a part of the landscape at this point as Kolos Hill or the statue of the Statesman with his arm raised in the Russian housing estate. The museum no longer interests anybody either. The school goes there every year on field trips from first grade up, but only because it's the only memorable sight in Boros, as long as you don't count visits from the circus, which, however, are unpredictable.

There, among the photographs of fish harvest festivals, with the whole village gathered in costume to celebrate, among the portraits of chieftains in traditional dress of fine leather with their favourite camels in embroidered bridles and a shabbily stuffed bear, Nami caught a familiar scent, the light aroma of wild oregano and honeydew melon. The bow, today a bright turquoise, drifting past the exhibits of traditional weaponry, of spears and harpoons of yew wood, scratches at the eczema on her hands and surreptitiously glances in his direction. Nami feels something akin to a deep longing, the aching, heart-wrenching desire of a stallion. The girl smiles at him and he quickly lowers his gaze. Searching the room for Alex with his eyes, he finds him where the largest crowds always gather in the museum–at the archival photographs of the original fisherwomen, who fished naked, using harpoons, and proudly displayed their catch on the pier. Every time he went on a field trip to the museum, Nami's gramma would wink and tell him to see if he could pick her out in the picture. He was always sure she must be pulling his leg, since none of the statuesque, well-endowed girls in the photo at the museum looked even remotely like his corpulent old gramma.

'Nobody fishes like this anymore,' the museum guide recites mechanically. 'Nowadays we have much more modern and efficient technology. Collective technology!

Does anyone here know why they made their spears out of yew wood?'

They all know. They've all heard it before many times. It only makes them all the more determined to keep their mouths shut.

'In any case, the fishing harvest in Boros has grown fifty times over in the past fifty years. That means we catch fifty times more fish now than your grandmothers used to catch,' says the guide, nodding her head up and down like a windup toy. She smiles wearily.

Nami's eyes search for the girl with the bow, but he no longer sees her in the spot by the wall. For a second he has the feeling his heart missed a beat, but then he realises how much freer he feels now that the girl is gone, almost as if someone had untied his hands.

'C'mon,' says Alex. 'Let's go outside. We can tear the legs off spiders or something.'

'Fifty times,' the guide repeats like a broken record.

Nami and Alex slink out of the museum, housed in a small building with flowers in the windows, which is reminiscent of a switchman's shanty, except for the large sign on the facade reading T WN SEUM. It's one of the few brick buildings in town that anyone still bothers to whitewash occasionally. The two boys lean against the wall between the windows.

'Fuck spiders, that's kid stuff,' says Nami. Alex, nodding solemnly, pulls a cigarette from his breast pocket and lights up.

'Who'd you nick that from?' says Nami, giving an astonished laugh. Alex, trying to look important, takes a puff and holds his breath, trying not to cough.

'Temptation's temptation, you know how it is,' says Alex, who is a good half a head shorter than Nami. Nami doesn't say anything, rubbing the eczema on his wrists.

'Did you hear about that thing that was born?'

'What thing?'

'That kid with three hands. To the chairman of the kolkhoz. His wife, I mean.'

Nami notices a fine, reddish growth of hair on Alex's upper lip.

'I thought it was a kid with no legs.'

'No, that was last time. Want a smoke?'

'That's okay.'

The two of them stand staring at the cluster of mining towers on the horizon. They look like dead trees.

'My mother got fired from the fish processing plant,' Alex says flatly. He draws up a gob of phlegm from his throat and hawks it far in front of him.

'Hm. What's she gonna do?'

Alex shrugs and purses his lower lip. 'Beats me. Something'll turn up, right?'

Nami nods.

'Should we go back in?'

'Fuck that.'

'Yeah, fuck it.'

They stand there a long time, leaning against the museum wall, gazing silently into the distance.

'That girl,' says Alex, clearing his throat after a while. 'That girl said for you to come meet her tonight at the port. I almost forgot.'

'What girl?'

'What girl do you think, genius. Guess she's got an itchy slit.'

'Jerk.'

'I would totally fuck her.'

'Well, I'm definitely not runnin all the way down to the port for her.'

***

The ships now sit so far away from the original port that the children have made a soccer field between the high tide line and the original port. The surface is on a bit of a slant, so whenever you pass the ball it tends to roll toward the water. It's impossible to run without stirring up dust, and every once in a while, someone's foot plunges through the stiff crust of sediment. Abandoned concrete piers covered with rotten algae jut from the hardened sand and mud, trash litters the ground beneath the mooring rings. The only pier that runs all the way to the fishing boats themselves is wooden; every six months the fishermen extend it a few metres further, so they won't have to walk across the parched lakebed with their fuel canisters and baskets of fish, and to give them somewhere to tie up their boats. A few small barges are scattered across the exposed lake bottom, their cracked hulls visibly decaying in the sun.

Nami lies on the dry grass overlooking a concrete pier, at the top of a hill where years earlier the Russians erected an antenna for interplanetary communications. At that time it was still taken for granted that they would fly to other planets, establish settlements, and hopefully join forces with the extraterrestrials. They even learned about it in Nami's school, but eventually the teachers stopped talking about it. The concrete pedestal was graffitied with symbols clearly meant to represent genitals, and the huge parabolic antenna bent a little closer toward the ground each year like a wilting sunflower. The paint was peeling off the ribs on the back of the dish in long, dark-red strips.

Nami lies twirling a blade of toxic grass in his mouth. The sun hangs low over the horizon, casting lengthy shadows. The dust filling the air covers clothing, chokes nostrils and lungs. A grungy stray dog creeps up through the grass and lies down near Nami. He has a large bump over his right eye. Nami flings a stone, chasing him away, and the dog trots off to lie down again at a safe distance.

Nami, glancing down at his hands, decides they look untidy and begins cleaning the dirt from underneath his nails. Peering off toward the city, he sees the girl on the road. The golden aureole of dust rising up around her makes her look a little like a spectre or a ghost. Nami goes on cleaning his nails, pretending not to see her. His mind is made up to let her pass without a word. His bowels are constricted and his stomach aches the same way it does after swimming in the lake.

The girl catches sight of him and shyly raises her hand in greeting. He nods. The girl agilely pushes off the concrete wall and swings herself up. Walks through the dry grass toward Nami, flip-flops slipping in the dust. She sits down next to him.

'You'll get your dress dirty.'

She waves her hand dismissively.

'Seems kind of silly, wearing a white dress around here,' Nami says, feeling like he's choking. He starts to cough. 'What with the dust and all,' he explains.

The girl clicks her tongue at the dog, who starts slinking toward them through the grass.

'Don't do that. He's nothing but fleas and ulcers.'

'I feel sorry for him. Look at how alone he is.'

The girl is sitting to the west of Nami, so he can see the fine hairs covering her neck and arms turning gold in the sunlight. He rolls onto his belly.

The girl clears her throat. 'Ehem, ehm. I'm Zaza.'

'Nami.'

'I know.'

'Really?'

'Of course. Everyone knows who you are.'

'What do you mean, everyone?'

'Are you kidding?' says Zaza, looking a bit startled.

'Oh, never mind. It's just that that time I saw you at the bus stop ... oh, whatever, it doesn't matter!' He spits out the blade of grass and plucks a new one. He hopes she doesn't notice that his fingers are trembling.

'You've got nice eczema,' he adds in an offhand way.

'What do you mean?' Zaza frowns.

'Just like most people's is all red and puffy, but yours is like sort of ... rosy. It's cute.'

'Oh.'

'I hope you don't take it the wrong way.'

'I rub it with lard. But it doesn't seem to help much.'

'I heard there was a baby born with three hands.'

'Yeah, there's two-headed lambs born all the time, but three-handed babies? We haven't had that before,' Zaza sighs. 'As soon as I finish school, I want to get out of here.'

He nods. 'Maybe we could go together.'

Zaza smiles and nods.

'So I'll come back tomorrow, okay?'

'Okay.'

Nami watches her walk away through the dusk. It's all he can do not to reveal the geysers of joy erupting inside him. Beyond the dry docks in the distance, he sees a home surrounded by piles of junk and a man in a diving suit moving around the garden with a dancer's grace. Nami tosses his head. The antenna's wires flap against the corroding dish in the wind. Maybe the aliens were finally transmitting a message. Nami concentrates on the rhythm, but he can't decipher it. His erection is still there.

***

Alex brings over something from the Russians, pages torn from a colour catalogue. There are women in underwear, smiling into the lens and pursing their lips. He trades it to Nami for a box of flare gun cartridges that Nami found in an unlocked army jeep. From the outhouse behind his gramma's house, all Nami can see through the round cut-out in the door is the patch of land where he carts the privy's foul-smelling contents each year in spring. The out-house itself is full of cobwebs and old newspapers. Inside, Nami leans against the dirty wall thinking of Zaza, with one hand holding the pictures of plump Russian women in underwear, with the other masturbating, when suddenly he hears a screech.

'You can't see!' cries the baker's wife as Nami's gramma bumps the back of her hand into the basket while they're peeling pole beans together. The purple beans go rolling across the table covered in colourfully patterned linoleum.

'Shh!' says Nami's gramma, glancing around with a look of alarm. 'I can still see well enough to mend nets and take care of the boy. And besides, I happen to know you have a limp, so you be quiet.'

The baker's wife just frowns, silently polishing the beans in the folds of her apron. Finally, after a long pause, she says, 'You're blind as a mole.'

'Try to say another word and I'll strangle you with your own scarf, you shrew,' hisses Nami's gramma. The baker's wife is on the verge of tears behind the loose wisps of grey hair falling down over her face, but she goes right on stubbornly polishing beans. But after a moment she stands up and bursts into tears, pouring her share of the beans into her apron and walking out without a word.

That same evening, Nami's gramma trips over the stoop and fractures her hip. Weeping in pain and softly cursing, she drags herself off to bed, which is where Nami finds her.

'I'll call the doctor,' he says, starting for the door, but his gramma yells that she would sooner break his legs than have a doctor look at her. Nami sits on the stoop, torn as to what to do. He's afraid to leave in case she gets worse, and afraid to go back in with her swearing and moaning in pain. He squeezes the fine dust up between his bare toes, piling it into heaps, and sinking dry stalks of grass into them. There's a wind starting to pick up. Nami sits on the stoop late into the night, then quietly steals inside.

'Give me a drink, boy,' his gramma whispers, and an icy chill comes over him. It sounds as if her voice is coming from beyond the grave, and she looks that way as well. Pale as a freshly whitewashed wall, she props herself up on one elbow, and even in the dark he can see the sweat glistening on her forehead. Nami pours her a ladle of water out of the bucket and watches as she gulps it down. There is a smell of illness and old age coming off her. Nami sits on the floor all night by his gramma's bedside, teeth chattering, sleeping only on and off. He wakes up every time she moans, though she is still silent for too long. When, toward morning, he finally manages to sink into a deep sleep, he is woken by the sound of loud male voices, followed by a pounding on the door.

Four men enter the house: the local doctor, the kolkhoz chairman, the school principal, and a fourth man, in a traditional shamanic headdress, but none of the other mention him or address him at any point. The baker's wife stands in the doorway, so agitated that she can barely breathe.

'What is it, dove?' Nami's gramma moans from bed. Her eyes shine feverishly.

'What is it, Grandma? How come you haven't gotten up yet? Did you decide to sleep in today?' the kolkhoz chairman jokes. He has sturdy shoulders, a swollen belly, and a shrunken behind.

'I guess I overslept,' Nami's gramma replies, her voice like a grater.

'All right, Granny, let's have a look,' the doctor says firmly, rolling back the duvet. He turns away as the stench of illness and sweat hits him in the face. However, he quickly recovers, adopting a benevolent expression as he leans in to examine Nami's gramma. He looks in her eyes and throat, then takes her pulse and temperature. When he touches the site of her fracture, she just hisses and bravely endures it. The man with the shaman's headdress remains standing behind the doctor's back.

'How old are you, Granny?'

'Fifty-four,' she whispers.

'No no no!' the baker's wife shouts from the door. 'It's been ages since she was that old! Liar!'

The doctor nods and gives the kolkhoz chairman a furtive wink. Then they all withdraw to the stoop, leaving only the man in the shaman headdress standing at the head of the bed. Nami sits quietly at the bedside, holding his gramma's feverish hand. It feels the same as the time he caught a bird and the little creature's heart was practically beating out of its chest.

'What's wrong, Gramma?' he whispers.

She gives no answer, breathing choppily in and out.

'Gramma?'

'Get me out of here, quick,' she whispers.

'What? Where should I take you? How?'

Nami hears a dark murmuring as the man in the headdress starts shifting his weight back and forth from foot to foot, singing and waving something over his head that looks like a gnawed bone.

'What is it, Gramma?'

Suddenly, as the shaman's voice rises in intensity, Nami's gramma starts to moan and howl like a wolf. Nami, plugging his ears in an effort to block out the cacophony, starts to rock backward and forward. As the wailing continues without let-up, he jumps to his feet and dashes out of the house. As he flies out the door, he slams into the baker's wife on the stoop. She staggers, bumping into the metal handrail and grunting heavily. Nami runs out to the garden and into the toolshed. He breathes in the smell of diesel fuel and counts to twenty. Then, picking up his grampa's carpenter's hammer, he proceeds to break several items, including a smoothing plane, some wooden wedges, and stakes for growing pole beans.

The day before, he and his gramma had had lunch out on the stoop. Eating melon together, juice dribbling down their chins, his gramma had laughed so hard to see how fast Nami's belly grew she nearly fell out of her chair. Holding the corner of her black apron in one hand, she wiped away the tears of laughter, shooing the wasps away with her other. Now a crowd gathered on their stoop, neighbours as well as people he was seeing for the first time. The men stood around closemouthed while the women twittered away, their children hanging off the fence overgrown with woodbine.

Nami steps out onto the stoop, jaw clenched, gripping the heavy hammer, and everyone falls silent.

The doctor stands at his gramma's bedside again, holding her hand. He is speaking to her in a quiet voice.

'What is it, Doctor?' Nami asks softly. 'What's wrong? Why are all these people here? She's just got a broken leg!'

'Yes, but ...'

'I had a broken leg too.'

'And how old were you?' says the doctor, smiling.

'I donno, six?'

'Well, there you go.'

The doctor sighs indulgently, shaking his head. Nami's

gramma lies with her eyes closed, breathing rapidly. No matter how urgently Nami pleads, she gives no response.

'You aren't going to send her to the lake, are you?' Nami shrieks. 'Not yet! She's still healthy! Gramma!'

A metal stretcher carried by the ambulance driver from the medical centre bangs against the door frame. People clear a path as if making way for some high-ranking official. The din of conversation gradually ceases.

'We gave her sedatives. What do you think we are, animals?' the doctor tells Nami angrily. 'Now step aside!'

Nami takes a step toward the doctor, raising the hammer over his head. The doctor coolly sizes him up.

'So what're you going to do, son?'

Nami fixes the doctor with a stare. Then suddenly his chin starts to shake uncontrollably and the hand with the hammer droops to his side. The doctor pushes him out of the way and the ambulance driver loads his gramma, groaning, onto the gurney. The crowd respectfully parts once again as the ambulance driver wheels the stretcher out the door.

***

The wind is picking up. The pier is overflowing with hundreds of townspeople; some have already fallen off the side onto the dry lakebed. The women clasp flowers in their arms, the men peer solemnly up at the sky, then down again at the lake; everyone is waiting for some sort of instructions. A flatboat with no oars, festooned with colourful ribbons, tosses in the waves, bumping against the fishing boats. Nami's gramma lies inside, forehead bedewed with sweat, blue ribbon tied around her eyes. Her hands, folded across her chest, are trembling, Nami notices.

The administrator nods his head and the shaman starts

murmuring darkly. Next, the women add their voices, joining in at a higher pitch. Eyes shining with moisture, they toss their flowers onto the old woman in the boat. It is a sad scene. The flowers are mostly withered at this time of year, their petals wilted or splotched with brown. The tugboat starts up its engine.

Nami squeezes through the people at the edge of the pier and jumps into the boat. It rocks wildly from side to side. Nami, ignoring the yells of the men on the pier, leans over his gramma and shouts so she can hear him over the rumbling engine and gusting wind.

'How can I stop this, Gramma? I'm coming with you, okay?'

His gramma grasps his hand, pulls it down to her face, and kisses it.

'You can't stop it, dove. Everything has to be as it is, to keep the Lake Spirit from being angry. He's still angry with us.'

'Gramma.'

'My sweet dove.'

'What'm I going to do?'

'You'll be just fine.'

'Does it hurt?'

'Eh.'

'I brought you some chardonnay.' He presses a half-litre bottle of moonshine into her hands and kisses her on the forehead.

'Thank you, dove. Thank you.'

She bursts into tears.

'Go now, Nami.'

Nami jumps out of the boat and swims back to shore through the mauve roses' carmine blossoms. His mouth is full of blood from biting the inside of his cheeks. As Nami wades ashore, the tugboat chugs away from the pier and the festooned flatboat disappears in a puff of diesel smoke. As the smoke clears, the boat with Nami's gramma inside can be seen reluctantly trailing behind, bumping over the waves as though it might capsize at any moment. The tugboat pulls it two hundred metres or so out into the lake, then unhooks it and heads back to shore. As the flatboat drifts off toward the horizon, the men on the pier pour out their shot glasses in honour of the Spirit of the Lake, then walk away in silence. Nami doesn't turn to look back at the boat again. He's angry. He feels his gramma should have told him something before she went away, something essential that he could use in life. He goes to the henhouse and cuts the throat of one of the three remaining hens.

***

Nami has dark, wild dreams, from which he is woken with a start by a door banging on the ground floor. His heart practically leaps from his chest. Where is he? What season is it? Where is his gramma? Why doesn't the kitchen smell of freshly fried doughnuts?

He sits up in bed, holding his head in his hands as reality slowly sinks in. As he drags himself downstairs, he realises he's drenched in sweat. He even stinks to himself. Standing in the middle of the kitchen is the kolkhoz chairman's spindly wife, cradling a child in her arms. She is surrounded by bundles of clothes and cardboard boxes.

'Good day,' she says, nodding shyly.

'You're going to live with us now, boy,' booms the chairman from behind her. The baby bursts into tears.

'Quiet, you freak, or I'll drown you in the lake!' the chairman laughs, then turns to carry the bundles upstairs.

Meanwhile his wife prepares tea. When her husband returns, he plops himself down at the table and rests his feet on a chair, still in his boots. He takes a sip of tea and shakes his head disapprovingly. 'That is one hell of a mess you've got out there in the garden, boy. Gonna take you a lot of work to make it presentable again. Guess your gramma should've kept a tighter rein on you, huh?'

A vein stands out on Nami's forehead, but he keeps his thoughts to himself. The baby starts crying again.

***

The first time Nami sees the baby undressed, he can barely keep from screaming in horror. It has a third hand growing out of the middle of its chest, a wrist and a palm with five little fingers wiggling like worms in a can. The hand itself is no more coordinated than the hands at the end of its arms. Still, he is a happy child, smiling back when Nami smiles at him and searching Nami out with his eyes whenever he's in the room.

Nami often takes the baby onto his lap, rocking and bouncing him up and down till the child squeals for joy. Sometimes he even plays with him by shaking his third hand, and the two of them shriek with laughter. The child sleeps with his mother in Nami's bed now, so Nami lies on the floor in the kitchen where his gramma's bed used to be. Her bed is occupied by the kolkhoz chairman, who snores as loudly as Nami's gramma used to snore. At least it gives him a feeling of security at night.

After a few days of digging the garden, Nami has calluses and sore muscles from using the spade and hoe. Sometimes he has to stay home and work the garden instead of going to school, but that doesn't bother him. The chairman's wife treats him kindly, saying 'Good day' and 'Good night' and giving him a playful wink from under her scarf every now and then. She may be skinny and ugly, but she has a pretty singing voice. Whenever she sings to the baby, Nami sits nearby and listens. She doesn't cook as well as his gramma either, but at least he doesn't go hungry. The chairman and his wife brought two goats with them when they moved in, so Nami enjoys fresh milk every evening, though it comes at the cost of his having to milk them, and sometimes even drive them out of the kitchen, which the goats are fond of visiting; whenever they manage to get inside, they climb up on the table and bleat at Nami triumphantly. Then the kitchen smells of goat for hours afterwards.

Nami clears out of the house every evening, saying that he's going to the beach to gather driftwood. Then he and Zaza walk back and forth over the dry lake bottom, picking up the occasional dry branch or piece of planking. Every now and then they come across a rubber boot, and once they even found a gold medallion. It was just a trinket, but neither of them knew the difference, so Zaza put it on a string and wore it around her neck. They held hands as soon as they were out of sight from shore but were still too shy to look each other in the eye. When they crossed paths on their way to school in the mornings, they locked eyes only fleetingly, then both lowered their gaze.

Nami also began seeing less of Alex, since the more he thought about him, the stupider he seemed.

***

'Where were you?'

Nami remains silent. Not out of defiance. He simply hasn't heard.

'I said, where were you!' the kolkhoz chairman roars.

Nami's thoughts are still in the clearing among the bushes, where he finally gathered up his courage to touch Zaza on the breast. He did so without warning and seemingly unintentionally, stepping up to her from behind and wrapping his right hand around her right bosom. She still wasn't too well endowed yet, but so what. For a moment she froze, and even stopped talking, but she left his hand where it was, making no attempt to slip free. Then she cleared her throat and picked up right where she had left off: 'So but she was ragged as a pair of old galoshes when she came home from the capital ...' Nami could feel the frenzied rush of her heart beating under his palm and he was happy.

'On the beach, gathering wood. Where else?'

Slap.

'You haven't brought home a thing!'

'The beach was already picked clean.'

Second slap.

'I won't have you making an ass of me. Where were you?'

Nami combatively raises his chin. 'That's my business.'

'Where were you? I'm asking for the last time.'

'What the fuck's it to you?'

Nami isn't expecting the fist to his stomach. The impact of the blow doubles him over at the waist.

'Where were you?'

'You're a bad man!' Nami wheezes. 'That's why the Spirit gave you a freak!'

The chairman slugs him in the shoulder. Nami hits the ground. Then in one well-practiced motion, the chairman pulls his belt from his pants and starts laying into him.

'You ungrateful little runt! After all the bad luck you've brought around here, you think you can teach me a lesson? Take that, you filthy brat! Let's see how you like the taste of blood!'

Even as the words leave the chairman's lips, Nami can feel his mouth filling with blood. Though the adrenaline keeps the pain at bay for the moment, he knows it won't be long before it starts to hurt bad. He runs his tongue over a chipped incisor.

The chairman's wife stands in the doorway, holding the crying baby in her arms. 'Borek,' she says in a placating tone.

Her husband, out of breath and dripping wet, lets go the belt. He stands over Nami, squinting in rage. The pungent scent of sweat rises off him.

'Now, where were you?'

Nami, flat on his back, panting for air, folds his hands across his chest.

'You stink of shit.'

The chairman gapes in disbelief, then delivers a weary kick to Nami's chest.

'You're nothing but a pile of shit. Just like that motherfucker who humped your bitch-ass mom!'

The chairman strides out of the house, carelessly shoving past his wife. Nami tries to get up, but his body is in too much pain.

'Sing to me,' he whispers to the woman. She turns and walks away.

Lying on the ground, Nami can feel the autumn wind creeping into the house through the cracks. The lash marks on his skin burn as if someone had sprinkled cinders on him.

The chairman carries him out to the henhouse and locks him in for the night. It's dark and cold and smells awful. Nami shakes with cold and rage. The agitated hens cluck and flap their wings.

***

The next morning Nami is allowed to return to the house. He is so stiff he can't even speak. The chairman's wife tries to serve him a bowl of oatmeal, but the chairman stops her.

'From now on, he only eats bread till he learns to behave himself.'

Even though it's so hard it crunches between his teeth, Nami is grateful just to be chewing a few dried crumbs of bread.

'And he will learn, isn't that right?'

Nami nods, his hands trembling uncontrollably. The windowpanes shake as a transport of military equipment passes by not far away.

***

Nami puts up with it a week. He digs the patch of land until his calluses ooze blood. Plays with the three-handed child and pines for Zaza. Sometimes when the chairman is away, his wife slips Nami a piece of meat or a doughnut. She doesn't say a word and Nami accepts it in silence.

Then one day the chairman catches him eating lentil soup. He kicks the chair out from under him so fast, Nami's teeth crack against the plate.

'Ungrateful ugly wench!' the chairman hisses through his teeth, hitting his wife so hard she collapses to the ground. Holding her face, she slides across the floor on her behind, into the corner.

'You better remember who feeds you and that little monster of yours,' the chairman says. 'Man shows his wife mercy, and the minute he turns his back on her, she's right there with the knife.'

'Forgive me, Borek.'

The chairman nods magnanimously.

• 'To the henhouse with you,' he tells Nami. 'Obviously one lesson wasn't enough.'

***

Now Nami is locked in the henhouse for good. He shares his water with the two hens and eats whatever leftovers the chairman's wife brings out from the kitchen. He no longer goes to school, instead spending his days sitting with his back against the wall, getting used to the smell of hen droppings and looking out through the cracks in the roof boards. The hens are uneasy at first, but after a few days they adapt to having him around. One day Nami overhears the squeaky voice of his teacher, asking if the chairman knows where he might be. The chairman affably replies he has no idea where the little runt has run off to—he takes after his mother, you know how it is. The teacher giggles and tells the chairman to make sure Nami comes back to school the minute he returns. He's her smartest pupil and morale in class isn't the same without him. The chairman, surprised, asks if she's sure she has the right person. The teacher just gives another playful giggle, at which point Nami realises the chairman is probably groping her ass, like he does to all the women in town who let him get away with it.

Come evening, Nami lifts the henhouse door off its hinges, sneaks out across the patch of land, and heads down to the port to meet Zaza. The number of minutes they have for their frenzied touching shrinks by the day, since Zaza has to be home before nightfall. Every night Nami comes home aching with desire, sniffing the melony scent of Zaza on his hands, and once darkness falls he steals into the pantry and eats whatever he finds there. One night the chairman's wife catches Nami in the act, mouth full, wolfing down food as fast as he can. She observes him in silence, one hand clasped in the other. Noticing her, Nami puts an index finger to his lips and the woman nods to signal her assent. She allows him to go on eating, calmly continuing to watch, then lets him out and locks the pantry door behind him. As he passes her, the woman strokes his shoulder. She tries to reach his head, but Nami has grown too tall. Then she digs into her pocket and pulls out a lollipop, a sugar rooster stuck to its cellophane wrapper, and surely tasting of violets and burnt sugar. Nami shakes his head. The chairman's wife, still smiling, returns the lollipop to her pocket. She'll give it to the child with the three hands tomorrow.

***

When the kolkhoz chairman leaves the house to oversee the ploughing and autumn planting, Nami creeps out of the henhouse and sits in the sun. He watches as the engineers and their families depart the housing estate, loading up their Zhigulis and Jeeps with backpacks and bags and paintings of birch groves, and disappear down the road in a cloud of dust without looking back. He sees his classmates as they walk to school, and he sees Zaza, which makes his insides knot up a little. With the weather turning cooler and the days growing shorter, the henhouse is starting to get cold at night.

He and Zaza will soon have to stop seeing each other, as nightfall keeps getting closer and closer to the time when school lets out. He squeezes her feverishly in his arms while she talks almost incessantly, smoothing out her skirt or tucking a fidgety strand of hair behind her ear. There's something sleepy about her. Nami kisses her on the eyes, the ears, the neck, his insides tightening up from the tension that can't be relieved. Pressing Zaza up against the pedestal of the interplanetary transmitter, he gropes up and down her thigh. She lifts her skirt even as she continues her story about the schoolchildren's forays into the abandoned apartments at the housing estate. Even before the tenants moved in, they were already destroyed, and there are newspapers in their windows now instead of broken glass.

Nami's face is buried deep in Zaza's tiny cleavage. As Zaza timidly strokes his penis, Nami can hardly stand it, choking, suffocating, it's more than he can bear. Still dizzy as he slowly raises his head to take a breath and save himself, he sees two Russian soldiers with rifles, one short and dark-skinned, the other a pudgy blond, wearing a kind-hearted look as he chews the nail on his right thumb. Zaza hisses softly, then briefly stops breathing. This is it. This is what every good mother warns her daughter about before she goes to sleep at night: Whatever you do, watch out for Russian soldiers. They're as dumb as three kopecks and horny from dawn to dusk. Run into them on a side street and you can bet you won't come out of it with your chastity intact.

'Nami,' says Zaza under her breath.

The short dark soldier gestures with the head of his rifle to indicate she should lift up her skirt. So simple, it's clear to everyone at once.

'Nami.'

Nami stands firmly clenching his jaw and squeezing his fingers into his palm.

'C'mon, let's go,' he says, taking Zaza by the hand. The two of them turn toward home, showing the sergeants their back. They take two steps, then hear the sound of a gunshot. The short dark soldier firing into the air. In Boros, you hear gunfire practically every day: sometimes it's training exercises, sometimes a lack of discipline, and sometimes just soldiers getting drunk and playing Russian roulette. Sometimes they shoot each other, or some new recruit puts a bullet through his head on the night shift. Whatever the case, it definitely doesn't cause a stir when there's shooting in town. Everyone just goes right on weeding their flower beds or gutting fish without so much as raising their eyes.

Nami and Zaza stop. They can each feel each other's hands shake. The vibrations meet in their fingertips, reinforcing the tremor. Zaza lets go of Nami's hand and, without even looking back, hitches up her skirt. The short dark-skinned man presses up against her from behind and squeezes her breasts. Zaza's eyes are shut tight, her chin quivering.

'Keep a lookout, Seryozha,' says the short dark soldier, and Seryozha, the good-natured tub of lard, nods. He holds the Kalashnikov casually under his right arm, finger on the trigger, gnawing at his thumb. Nami closes his eyes and pictures himself in a single motion kicking the rifle out of the fat soldier's hand and knocking him to the ground, then forcing the other bonehead to kneel and shooting his dick to a pulp. What he sees when he opens his eyes is Zaza's bobbing white breasts with their dark areolas and the sergeant's brown-skinned buttocks pumping back and forth, the left one with an ugly birthmark that looks like a melon cut in half. Nami squeezes his head between his hands like he's trying to break it open. It feels like his eyes are going to burst from their sockets, but that's it. He covers his ears to keep from hearing Zaza's cries. Only she isn't crying out. Totally silent, eyes closed, Zaza bites down on the corners of her mouth, but not a single groan escapes her lips.

'Did you get a good look, twerp?' the soldier says as he climbs off Zaza. He glances down at his member, gives it a proud slap, and tucks it back inside the pants of his grubby uniform.

'Come on, Seryozha. Your turn,' he says, beckoning to his companion. Seryozha, blinking nervously, undoes his pants. Nami takes advantage of the momentary distraction and fires off like a rocket, tumbling down the slope and weaving through the trees until he reaches the edge of the forest where the dirt road passing through town comes to an end. He knows the Russians won't dare shoot at him as long as he can reach the port. He knows if he caught a glimpse of Seryozha's erect penis he would choke on his own bile.

'Nami!' he hears Zaza calling from behind him.

***

For the next few days, Nami leaves the henhouse only at night. He has trouble sleeping. Every time he closes his eyes, he sees Zaza's milky white breasts bobbing up and down. It disgusts him–Zaza disgusts him. He feels a constant need to wash; every night he sneaks out to bathe in the icy lake; his skin only itches even more, his eczema getting worse. The nights are cool; mornings, the drinking trough is covered in ice. Nami clutches the hens against him for warmth. They don't resist.

'It's cold out here,' Nami says as the kolkhoz chairman steps through the door with a handful of gnawed bones.

'Sure is,' the chairman says with a nod, drawing himself upright.

'I'm not staying here anymore,' Nami says. The note of determination in his voice captures the chairman's attention.

'I said I'm not staying here in the henhouse anymore,' he repeats, but the chairman just makes a face. 'I go out every night, since you're such a loser you can't even lock the door right, plus I'm banging your wife,' Nami says quietly. 'I could leave whenever I want and go straight to the police. The day they found out that you had me locked up, they would put you on a flatboat and send you to the Spirit. Any night I wanted, I could've burned the house down over your head.'

Nami glowers, the chairman staring back without a word.

'I'm not staying one more day in this stinking henhouse,' Nami says again. After all the weeks he's spent here, he can feel himself starting to choke on the smell. He rubs his wrists feverishly. The thought of leaving the house where he grew up makes the blood rush to his head. He feels like his eyes are bulging out of their sockets.

'I give you my blessing,' the chairman says quickly. 'Leave this henhouse and never return.' Nami gives a nod of agreement and tears the door off its hinges. Then he bows his head and follows the chairman outside. The sky is grey, the air cool. When Nami was little, by this time of year it had already snowed, and he and the other kids would go sledding on the hill above the school. Now there hadn't been any snowfall in several winters, just like there was no more rain in spring or fall anymore.

'I'm leaving Boros,' Nami says, letting out a deep breath.

'Good idea,' says the chairman.

'I can come back to my house whenever I want. And I need money.'

'All right,' the chairman says. He pulls his wallet from his pocket and takes out a few bills for Nami. As Nami reaches out for them, the chairman suddenly pulls the bills back to his chest and asks, 'Did you really sleep with my wife?'

Nami smiles and shakes his head. 'Are you kidding? She's ugly as a thief.'

The chairman frowns, then nods his head and hands over the money. It isn't much, but it's the first time Nami has ever held banknotes in his hand. They're red and green and worn from excessive handling.

'How come you didn't leave sooner?' the chairman asks, shaking his head.

Nami just shrugs. There's no way he can ever explain to the chairman how hard it was to give up the everyday pleasure of being with Zaza. His lungs tighten at the thought. He enters the house and packs some of his things—a knife for gutting fish, two books from the school library and his school ID, a photo of the capital he had clipped from a magazine, a certificate for second place in a recitation competition, a spare shirt and dress pants, a comb, and the pages torn out of the women's underwear catalogue–in his grampa's kit bag that he used to take with him on field trips. Nami is glad the woman with the three-handed baby is gone so he doesn't have to tell her goodbye.

'Write it down,' he says to the chairman.

The chairman, sitting at the kitchen table holding his head in his hands, suddenly jerks in his seat. 'What?'

'Write down that I'm leaving the house with your blessing and that when I come back it'll be just as much mine as yours.'

'You are one sly sonuvabitch.'

'Write.'

Labouring to his feet, the chairman reaches up and takes a sheet of paper from a stack on a shelf above the window weighted down with a stone. He sits back down at the table and thinks it over a long time, then writes a few sentences, signs at the bottom, and folds the document in thirds. Nami stands spread-legged over the chairman, slurping clean water straight from the ladle till it dribbles down his chin. It tastes a little sour. He loads one of his pockets with hard-boiled eggs from the breadbasket on the table and fills the other with raisins from a bowl prepared as a snack for the child. He unfolds the sheet of paper, reads it through carefully, and makes a frowning face.

'Not good enough,' Nami says. He reaches into the oven for a pan of roast meat, then proceeds to polish it off, loudly smacking his lips, while the chairman sweats over his rewrite. Nami reads through the new version and, finding it satisfactory, he stuffs the sheet of paper into the pocket of his grampa's thick sheepskin coat, which still hangs on the back of the door.

'You're nothing but a whelp, and every other grown-up who isn't a nice guy like me is gonna wipe their ass with you. You won't even get to the end of town.'

'You've got chicken shit on your shirt,' Nami says without even looking at him. He puts on his grampa's coat and discovers it's too small. His chin is greasy.

The chairman sweeps aside the junk littering the table in front of him—a yellow glass salt shaker, a bottle of soda, his glasses, a newspaper, farm financial statements, a torn strip of flypaper—and lays down his head. His breathing is heavy and loud.

His wife materialises out of nowhere like a ghost and gently rests a hand on his shoulder.

'Is the Spirit angry, Borek? Is that why you let him leave?'

'Shut up,' the chairman says, lunging at her angrily. She barely jumps back in time.

***

The sheepskin coat is tight and bulky, but at least it keeps him warm. It's the first time in days Nami hasn't felt cold. He walks alongside the road instead of on it, last year's withered grass crunching beneath his feet. Apart from that, he is surrounded by winter silence, the distant lapping of the lake the only sound he hears. He sees the young girls pouring out of the girls' school in a colourful mass, grey coats topped by yellow, white, and turquoise hats, and something wrenches inside him. He quickly averts his gaze, not wanting to know if Zaza is among them. On his tongue he can taste the sour tang of bile. He sprinkles a few raisins in his mouth and sucks on them long and hard, rolling them around on his tongue. From a distance he can see that the Statesman has lost his waving right hand, and that makes him happy.

There are just a few regulars sitting around the nonstop. The door is closed and everyone is inside. A grey-blue cloud of smoke hovers at the height of Nami's chest. The barmaid sings softly to herself behind the counter, feet resting on a stool, lips painted with lipstick as red as a fatal wound. She glances at Nami indifferently.

'Where are you on your way to, dove?'

'I'm going to the capital.'

'Nothing keeping you here, huh?'

Nami shrugs.

'I'm sorry about your gramma. She was a good woman.'

Nami nods.

'Cup of coffee?'

'Sure.'

The barmaid slowly stands and puts the water on to boil.

'You're doing the right thing, dove. This is an awful place. I'd go with you myself if I could.'

Nami shivers.

'I would. I should've left. But now I'm stuck here for good.'

'Hey, Marina! Lay off the kid and give us a drink!' shouts one of the regulars sitting around the table.

'Ah, shut your mouths,' Marina says, waving them off.

The men grumble, but they don't dare protest. Marina pours some coffee into a tin mug, adds a few drops of liquor, stirs it in, and hands the mug to Nami. Her cheeks, large and red, are riddled with burst veins.

'That'll warm you up, dove. The road is long. But even if it takes you all the way across the lake, it's worth it to get out of here. Those Russian riffraff raped a girl again last night, did you hear?'

Nami shakes his head no and bends his face over the mug.

'It's always the same: they waylay some girl in the woods,

ruin her life, and no one ever punishes them, since our cops and courts don't have any power over them. Nothing but a bunch of stupid pricks!'

Marina sighs, opens the cash register, and hands Nami three bills.

'There you go–from me.'

'That sure is an awful lot.'

'You got a problem with that?' she screams.

'I'm sorry,' whispers Nami. He takes the money and buries it in the pocket of his coat.

'You think there's someone out there waiting for you with open arms? Save it for when you need it. C'mere.'

Nami leans across the counter, and Marina grabs him by the scruff of the neck and plants a kiss on his forehead. It's the dry kiss of an old woman, smelling of onions and lost self-respect.

'Pavel!' she exclaims as she straightens back up.

One of the regulars turns to look. Bald-headed with broad shoulders and crude tattoos on his forearms.

'Any chance you're heading to the capital anytime soon?'

The bald man nods. Marina walks to his table and, hands on her hips, negotiates with him for a while. Points to Nami, nodding her head. Raises her voice a couple of times, but Nami still can't understand. The bald man stares at him searchingly through the cloud of smoke, then finally throws up his hands in surrender.

'Pavel's sailing a tanker to the capital tomorrow morning. He'll take you on board.'

'Oh boy!'

'Yeah, yeah. He owes me, so it worked out.'

'Thank you, Auntie.'

Marina snorts in disgust.

'Spare me the auntie crap.'

Pavel waves to the boy, so Nami picks up his kit bag and

his still hot cup of bad coffee and moves to the bald man's table. Resting his hairy forearms, covered in pictures of mermaids and the name Natali, against the plastic tablecloth, Pavel glowers from under a pair of bushy joined eyebrows. Toward morning he lays his head on the table to take a nap, but the whole rest of the evening and all through the night, Nami doesn't hear him say a single word.

It's still dark out as the two of them leave the nonstop together. Whatever humidity is left in the air turns to frost on the gravel as they walk downhill to the port. Nami skips along like a bouncing ball, while Pavel moves cautiously, as if trying to keep the alcohol in his body from spilling over the edge. As he walks unsteadily across the wooden pier, Nami trails in his wake, fighting the urge to prop the bald man up from behind. When they get about halfway down the length of the pier, Pavel lays down on the boards without a word, pulls the hood of his bleached red fishing jacket over his head, and shuts his eyes. Nami shivers with cold; he can feel it creeping under his nails.

'C'mon, Pops, get up,' he says gingerly, but Pavel doesn't stir. Nami remembers the way his gramma used to wake his grampa when he came home in that state and collapsed in front of the doorstep: adopting the tone of an officer, she would roust her husband with a series of clear and loud commands and chase him into the house. 'Drunks need to be told what to do,' she would sigh to the drowsy-eyed Nami as she herded his grampa to bed.

'Get up!' shouts Nami. Pavel just sleepily snuffles.

'Get up, you lazy bum!'

Pavel starts scratching around on all fours, then slowly and gingerly gets to his feet. He staggers but remains standing.

'Onto the ship with you, you bunch of turds!' Nami yells, and Pavel springs into motion, squinting uncertainly in the dawn, but he heads in the right direction, and it looks like he'll be able to stay within the two-metre-wide wooden pier without falling off. Nami follows behind with a weary smile. As Pavel steps into the motorboat, for a moment it looks like he'll make it, but then he wobbles, trips, and falls into the narrow strip of cold water between the boat and the pier. Nami sits on the pier, watching awhile as Captain Pavel attempts to climb on board. His movements are efficient, virtually automatic, no needless splashing or cursing, not a trace of his previous drunkenness. Nami hops down from the pier into the motorboat, and after a few moments of puffing and exertion, together they manage to slide Pavel back aboard.

'Thanks,' says Pavel. 'You can untie us.'

Pavel starts up the engine and, almost without even looking, steers the boat toward the silhouette of a red and black oil tanker anchored on the east side of the bay. Neither of them says a word, the thrum of the engine and the waves dashing against the boat the only sound. Pavel sniffles. His nose is running and water drips from his hair. Nami curls up in back and watches the receding town of Boros turning pink in the dawn as it climbs out of the darkness. The outline of the parabolic antenna for communicating with aliens slowly melts away on the horizon. Nami's teeth chatter with cold. Everything is pink.

***

Nami leans over Zaza's white body, feeling the blood rush to his temples. Zaza smiles, clasping his head in her palms. Nami takes her nipple into his mouth and Zaza lets out a sigh as the colour drains from her face. Nami's pulse quickens to the point he can no longer stand it. He moves his head down Zaza's body, lower and lower, until he's between her legs. His chin bumps up against something hard—a concrete wall like a dam has sprung up in front of him. Zaza moans, for God's sake, whatever you do, just don't stop. Her face is pale and she's foaming at the mouth. Nami claws at the wall frantically till he manages to find a door, presses down on the handle, and to his surprise it opens. Stepping through the door, he finds himself in a long hallway, lit only by a feeble light at the other end. He runs and runs, but the longer he runs the farther away the end of the hallway seems to get.

Then he gets the idea of putting his thumb in his mouth, like he used to do as a child, and suddenly he's standing at the far end of the hallway, gazing out at the mound of Venus. He realises his heart is pounding. The downy pubic hairs are joyfully standing on end, and Nami is joyful too. Just then, he detects a movement in the undergrowth; he rubs his eyes, but no, he isn't imagining it – little black spiders stream from the clump of pubic hair, whole hordes of them crawling over each other's backs, pouring out like an oil strike, gushing uncontrollably. Nami recoils and shrieks in terror. The flood rushes toward him, and he sprints back down the dark corridor, screaming as he feels the spiders underneath his shirt.

Nami wakes up to find that he's sobbing aloud. There's a smell of diesel in the air and the sound of the engine's monotonous drone. He lies on the floor in the engine room, rocking like a buoy on the surface, feeling like he's about to hurl at any moment. His head is pounding and he's burning up with fever.

***

He has wild dreams, twitching in his sleep. He shakes and trembles and drops of sweat trickle down his temples. The engine room's metal floor is broiling hot. In his more lucid moments, he thinks about his gramma in the flatboat, but he isn't sure if that was yesterday or a year ago. He sees his nose; it looks to him unfathomably large.

The ship slows down. Nami hears someone cry out, the crowing hoarseness of a weary man, most likely a command to the crew. He hears the scrape of the anchor chain, feels the anchor grate against the bottom. Propping himself up on an elbow, he sees a can full of water in front of him and thirstily downs it. A fluorescent light coughs on and off on the ceiling high overhead. The engine room has two levels, with a gallery down the middle. It thrums darkly. The instruments, walls, and pipes are all coated in a greenish paint, which is peeling off in places.

Nami sits up and sees the figure of Captain Pavel beside him. He looks unrested and unhealthy, his hair thick with grease.

'We're here,' he mumbles, the words barely intelligible. 'Run along.'

Nami nods. He can smell that his own shirt reeks of sweat. He gets to his feet too quickly and his head starts to spin. He staggers.

'Have you got somewhere to go?' Captain Pavel asks, giving him a searching look.

Nami shakes his head, and the world starts swaying again. He notices some posters of naked girls on the wall behind Captain Pavel. They have their butts stuck out and all of them are blonde.

'Look for the big bazaar. You can ask anyone. There's a park behind the bazaar. The job market is there.'

Nami nods. He has no idea what a job market is, but he knows he'll go there anyway, like a moth drawn to a glowing light in the middle of the night. As he stumbles up on deck, he breathes in the air and feels a little better. It's not fresh air—it smells of burnt diesel, garbage, and fish—but at least it moves. He can see the capital laid out before him. He's on the other side of the lake. His head starts spinning so badly, he nearly faints.

# II
# Larva

If Nami had to describe the city, he wouldn't know where to begin. With the buildings so tall here he finds himself instinctively crouching, and his eyes constantly search for the sky in between them. The air is filled with honking horns, backfiring exhausts, and shouting. A woman in a high voice chides her child for crying. There's an odour of faeces, sweet perfume, and frying fat. Grease-stained bits of paper and dust float through the air. The people here look a little different, too; their eyes are brighter and shinier, and they move faster. Even the street dogs are in more of a hurry. Colourful posters are plastered all over the walls in multiple layers. The ones underneath come unglued and trap the dust from the air.

Someone honks from behind him and Nami gives a startled jump. A girl with sunglasses on sits behind the wheel of an abnormally clean and shiny off-road vehicle. Her hair and teeth are as dazzling as the collection of bracelets on her hand with which she's gesturing. Nami just stands staring as the girl shouts and waves at him to clear the way. She has a picture of a seahorse on her rhinestone-studded T-shirt, and two large round, three-dimensional breasts underneath. Nami has a painful erection. Somebody shoves him out of the road and the girl in the white car honks and moves on. Nami stands staring after her for a long time, stroking his sternum. A middle-aged blonde with black roots snorts derisively. She has a spare tyre around her waist and a moustache over her upper lip.

'Could you tell me the time, Auntie?' Nami asks. He has no idea what time of day it is. The sun is fairly low, and there isn't a cloud in the sky, but the gusting wind has wound a cookie wrapper around his ankle.

'Auntie?' She gives him a look over the rims of her glasses, then bursts out laughing so hard it makes her belly jiggle. The golden teeth click in her mouth. Nami tilts his head to the side and watches until she stops laughing. Finally the woman sets her shopping bag down on the ground, takes off her glasses, and wipes the tears from her face.

'It's half past eight,' she says. She picks up her bag and turns to leave. 'Eight thirty, boy.'

'Thank you,' says Nami.

The woman turns her head and smiles. 'Would you like a pirogi?'

'Yes, please.'

'Yes, please? Some man you are. Get a grip on yourself!'

'It's just that I'm really hungry.'

'Follow me.'

The woman crosses the street. The wind blows cold now. Even in his grampa's sheepskin coat, Nami is shivering. The woman enters a glass door with a red neon sign on it. Most of the letters are missing, so Nami can't put together what it said originally: C – – – – K – – – – ER – – – M. K – – K – – H.

Stepping up to the dingy counter, the woman orders two meat pirogi for Nami and a black coffee for herself. She then watches without a word, smoking and nodding her head as the food disappears down his throat. Her fingernails are bright red, like the colour of kid goat's blood. The man behind the counter, in a grubby white cap, coughs neurotically, his belly brushing against the cash register. The pirogi taste of burnt oil and keep coming back on Nami for several hours afterward, along with the taste of bile.

As he carries the woman's bag of groceries up to the

third floor, his knees start to buckle. She waves wearily toward the elevator shaft, explaining that it isn't running and never has. They never even installed a car. Breathing heavily, she fumbles around in a large white purse, searching for the keys.

'Come in.'

A honey-coloured light shines in the hall on the other side of the door. Nami catches the scent of naphthalene balls, and the familiar smell makes his head spin a little. For a moment he's back in his gramma's closet, where he used to sit whenever he needed to hide from his drunken grampa, inhaling the scent of naphthalene and scratching at the lice on his head. The woman probably has warm milk and a soft bed with a fluffy duvet. She takes off her pink feather coat and changes into rubber slippers. As she hangs her coat on the hall stand, the overpowering scent of musk washes over Nami.

'Come on in,' the musk whoops cheerfully. 'What are you doing, standing there like a broken alder?'

Nami feels like he's going to faint. As a wave of weakness comes over him, he has to rest his head on the door frame.

'I need to go now,' he mumbles. 'Which way is it to the bazaar?'

'Just come relax,' says the musk, tilting her head to the side, spilling the fat beneath her chin. She reaches out her hand and takes a step toward him. Nami firmly shakes his head, pushing her away. He feels like he's choking on the musk. He starts to gag. He picks up his kit bag from the floor and bolts toward the door.

'You're a nutjob,' the woman says, shaking her head. 'Go ahead then.' Nami hears the door slam as he dashes down the stairs.

A moment later he's on the street. He sets off willy-nilly down the pavement. His step is light again, he's already feeling better. Occasionally he even jumps over the potholes in the pavement. At one point, he's joined by a dirty yellow dog, but the dog turns off to the right at the first intersection.

The air is cool and razor sharp. A gust of wind from who knows where carries the smell of diesel. Nami bumps into people as he stares into the shop windows, every so often stopping to listen to the city's noise. Several times he finds himself in the same spot where he had stopped a while earlier. And once he is startled to see his own reflection in the glass of a shoe store display; his lips are swollen and peeling. Nami engraves himself into the relief of the city. When his feet start to hurt and his fingers turn numb with cold, he sees the first stalls of the bazaar—potato crates, baskets filled with fish and red apples, jars of pickled vegetables and plastic dishes stacked with honeycombs. He smells the aroma of mutton on the grill and swallows dryly. Thundering music and high-pitched voices blast from several radios.

The stallholders at the bazaar have broad faces with deep wrinkles around their eyes, reminiscent of the cracks in the arid surface of the steppe, just like the inhabitants of Boros. Nami buys a cup of tea and a mutton cutlet. Tears spring to his eyes as the hot juice runs down his neck. He smiles like someone granted absolution.

'Where's the job market?' he asks the woman in the green scarf selling mutton cutlets. She nods in response, but her radio is on so loud he has to ask her two more times before she hears what he says. She waves vaguely in the direction of the crowds streaming into the bazaar. Nami wipes his hands on his coat, takes a deep breath, the cold air stinging his nose, and sets off.

After weaving through the stalls for another fifty metres or so, he reaches the edge of the marketplace. He can tell by the open waste containers full of rotten food. Across the street is a park. Well maintained, paths freshly swept, leaves raked into piles. A fountain stands at the entrance, apparently still in working order, though it's currently turned off in view of the low temperatures. Gracing the fountain is a statue of a water nymph holding a jug in one hand. In summer, water runs from the jug into a shallow pond where children can frolic and play in the heat, but apart from a shredded plastic bag the pond is empty now. The water nymph is garbed in a close-fitting tunic accentuating the outline of her breasts. Nami examines it with interest from every side, then throws on his backpack, noticing the sky has clouded over in the meantime.

On one side, a wall covered in woodbine forms a natural border to the park. Noticing a hole with bars along the wall, Nami goes closer and sees that it is a caged pen, apparently empty. Lying on the concrete floor are a can of Coca-Cola and a long stick with tooth marks all along its length. A dry tree trunk juts from the floor up to the ceiling. Nami looks up and sees a furry animal sitting at the top. It gazes at him apathetically, playing with its penis.

Suddenly Nami senses the presence of another person beside him. A man in a khaki hunting vest with a halo of curly silver hair.

'What is that?' Nami asks the man.

'A monkey,' the man says, dragging on his cigarette.

'Yeah, okay, but what kind?'

'Just a monkey,' the man says. 'His name's Majmun.'

'Majmun!' Nami calls, but the monkey doesn't take the slightest bit of interest in him. It just stays there on its branch, fiddling with its genitals. Then it turns around and shows Nami its red behind.

'Why is he here?' asks Nami.

'Why do you think?' the man says, throwing up his hands.

'It's a city park. When the kids come, they go first to the stone bear, then to the fountain, then to Majmun, and end with ice cream. Every Sunday.'

'Why does he keep holding his dick like that?'

The man in the hunting vest looks skyward and throws up his hands again. 'Boy. I don't know what to tell you. Because he can?'

Nami giggles.

'Majmun,' he calls again softly. The monkey still has his bottom ostentatiously turned to Nami. Nami's nose stings with the pungent scent of musk.

***

The job market consists of three, at times four lines of men, standing along the road. Dressed in all colours of misery, they reek with the common smell of humanity and unwashed underwear. Usually they are silent, staring resignedly down at the ground. Their overworked hands, permanently ingrained with dirt, are clenched into a fist. When a car drives by with a prospective employer, the men stand up straight and suck in their bellies. A hand reaches out the car window and beckons someone with a finger. Three or four men step out of line, run to the car, and start negotiating with the owner of the hand. After a brief shoving match, then one or two of the day labourers climb into the car and their spots in the first row are quickly filled by the foot soldiers from behind. A little way off to the right stands an army of women day labourers—cleaning ladies, gardeners, and babysitters. The sounds of low conversation and occasional laughter remind Nami of lying under the cherry tree in springtime, listening to the buzzing of the bees up above.

Nami gets in line at the end of the third row. Nobody picks him all afternoon. No prospective employer even looks at him. Nobody points their finger at him and asks how many bags of cement he can carry. At nightfall, the crowd slowly drifts away. Even with marching in place constantly, Nami is still cold to the bone. The woman he helped with her groceries would certainly give him a mug of tea and maybe also a clean bed, but just the memory of her pungent body odour and her rubber sandals squeaking makes Nami start shaking all over again.

He spends the night in front of Majmun's cage at the park. He doesn't sleep much, and only off and on, shivering with cold, but in the morning he wakes up fairly refreshed, though his ears and nose are frozen. When the stallholders appear and the market opens for business, Nami buys a cup of sweet black tea and a cabbage pancake. The day is a bit more friendly today, the sun attempting to break through the clouds, but a cold wind is blowing. Nami goes back to the job market again and shows up early enough to get a place in the second row. He recognises a few of the men's faces from the previous day. They nod to each other in greeting, then ignore one another for the rest of the day, except to hold somebody's place when one of them needs to urinate.

Nami calculates that the buyers take roughly one fifth of the available workforce every day. So five days should be enough. But it takes twice as long. He's running out of money, and every night the air gets a little chillier. He stinks to himself. His hair itches.

Then a man comes along in a pick-up and points to Nami and two other men. Without a single question, he loads them into the bed of his truck and takes them to a warehouse in the port to unload cargo from ships. It's hard labour; one of the men hired with Nami shatters his ankle during the very first shift. Nami has no gloves, and after just a few hours his hands are covered in bloody blisters. His back aches from lifting and carrying crates of carrots and onions. He can't believe the city has enough people to eat that many onions. They get a fifteen-minute break for lunch. The other men are trying to save money, same as Nami, so instead of lunch they just go out on the concrete pier and light up a smoke. They sit atop the wooden crates, puffing cheap cigarettes and gazing silently out at the lake.

Pools of red sulphur, a by-product of mining, sit drying up on the site where the lake once used to be. Over time it turns to a yellow substance that men in safety helmets cut into huge yellow slabs, which are then shipped to sulphur-hungry buyers in Africa and Australia. Flames shoot from four black towers in the background.

After a few days of agony, Nami begins to toughen up. His calluses harden, and though his back still aches, the pain recedes to the point that he no longer perceives it. After a week he gets his first pay cheque. Only half the promised amount, since the other half is deducted for housing. He has to be judicious with money—there's barely enough left over to eat—but he's trying to save up enough for new pants and a coat, so at least he won't feel like a villager. When the hunger gets to be too much, he chases it away by drinking lots of water. He has a vague feeling he ought to go out at least once a week and be with people who don't stink of fish and have dirt under their nails. Meanwhile somewhere in between his consciousness and subconsciousness, an indistinct figure appears. Though he doesn't recognise who it is, from the long hair and breasts he concludes that it must be a woman. He has a nebulous feeling he'd like to have her, but given the lack of clarity about what action he would need to take for that to happen, he puts the whole thing on hold.

The water in the dormitory runs only in the morning, if at all, and only cold. In the winter there is no heat. The plywood floor is slowly rotting away. The sour smell from the toilets permeates everything, seeping into the walls, his clothes, hair, pillow. The windows are filled with plywood panels instead of glass. Wind blows through the cracks. The beds are hard, though certainly softer than the withered lawn in front of Majmun's cage at the park. Nights are short. Nami wakes to the sound of footsteps from a co-worker whose shift starts even earlier than his.

Eleven other men live in the room together with Nami. They come home so tired that at night they just collapse into bed and fall asleep. They no longer even bother to put up a fight against the bedbugs. One day Nami lifts his mattress and sees thousands of them, all over the frame. The men don't have strength to argue or even masturbate. Every so often Nami thinks back to his time with Zaza, but any memories he has are mercilessly tainted by the image of the rhythmically swaying Russian behind, so he quickly dismisses them. His muscles are growing. He barely talks to the other men, apart from a few he exchanges greetings with in the washroom every morning.

One morning Nami wakes and before he even opens his eyes his whole body goes stiff. An awareness runs through his body, and he feels all his muscles tightening up. Even with his eyelids closed, the electric light from the bulb on the ceiling courses into his brain. With every pulse of blood, it feels like his fingers are growing longer then shorter again. His heart is pounding wildly. He doesn't even have to reach under the pillow to know the purple sock with his savings is gone. He presses his hand against the blanket, eyes still closed. He doesn't bother to look around, no one would tell him anything anyway. He was stupid; now the money he was saving to buy a coat is gone. From now on, the only place he'll put it is his boxers, where he'll keep it safely secured with a safety pin. He grits his teeth and waits it out in the dormitory till spring.

***

Now Nami works in sulphur production. He's still gluey-eyed as he walks through the dark to the factory site in the morning. He has no choice but to go on foot, since the buses don't go to the plant, and the factory truck only gives a ride to the skilled workers, who have been working in production so long that most of them suffer from emphysema. Nami is just a young, unskilled asphalt layer, so he walks to work from the dorm, hands jammed deep in the pockets of the shabby red ski jacket he bought at the bazaar; it may be second-hand, but it's warm. He and a group of other men walk together; hardly anyone speaks. Sometimes the residual moisture in the air creates a crust of ice on the uneven spots in the road that crunches under their factory-issue boots. The boots have a thick sole of hard rubber, but it doesn't take long for the hot asphalt to start to burn their feet, and it doesn't let up till the end of the shift. Nami is especially careful when it comes to his boots, since he won't get a new pair if he ruins these.

All day long, then, he walks behind a truck with hot asphalt flowing out of it. It makes Nami think of the blueberry syrup that his gramma used to make and pour over his pancakes. He breathes in the sweet smell of the liquid asphalt until it pervades his entire being. Spreads the asphalt using a wooden rake.

He walks home in the dark with a dusting of yellow sulphur on his jacket. Legs and lungs burning, he usually just collapses onto his bunk, not bothering with hygiene. Sunday is the only day he has time for that; assuming the water is running, he steps under the icy shower and washes away the week's filth, to stop stinking for a while. Borrowing a pair of scissors, he trims his toenails and fingernails and the hair growing over his ears. Then sets out into the city.

He has no one to ask, no one to turn to for advice. Nor does he know what to ask even; he doesn't know his mother's name or what she looks like. He doesn't even know if she's still alive. He's looking for a woman whose existence is as real as the Spirit of the Lake's.

He makes the rounds: the train station buffet, the market stalls, the tea rooms and upscale cafés (just peeking in from the door, from behind the heavy gold-pleated curtains), searching the women's faces for something that might ring a bell. For the most part, all he finds is indifference and smudged mascara. The women either ignore him or wave him off like they were shooing away a pesky fly. The place Nami likes to go best is the port, where sometimes he can meet people from his neck of the woods, sailors from the oil tankers and fishermen with deep salty wrinkles. He doesn't know how to talk to them, so he just sits at the table next to them, drinking Russian tea from a tall glass and listening as the men talk about torn nets and withered trees, about their moody women and how many neighbours have come down with cancer, and almost always about the last time they went to the brothel or their plans to go again.

After one bender, they take Nami with them. The Symfonie house of ill repute is an even more depressing place than its name suggests. Just inside the front door is something like a reception room, with a counter where a fat man in a tracksuit issues room keys while doubling as bartender. Weary girls lounge about on grubby, sagging divans. They don't look much like the ladies from the underwear catalogue; their thighs are dotted with cellulite and bruises, and their roly-poly bellies spill from under their short tops. At least some of them are sprouting moustaches. Cigarettes jut from their fingers, with long and colourfully painted nails.

Nami leans casually against the counter, contemplating

the girls with a worldly-wise look. Some of them are probably old enough to be his mother. He catches the eye of a girl in a powder-pink dress. She must be the youngest one here; she can't be much older than he is. The girl stares back at him with a look less alluring than tired, pleading. Nami leans across the counter, but just then the guy turns the music up to full blast, a shrill Middle Eastern disco song with wailing vocals, drowning out Nami's question about price. He doesn't bother to try a second time. The men, tossing back one shot after another, are drunk in not even half an hour. They start barking at the prostitutes, who come and sit on their laps, looking bored and annoyed. The girl in the powder-pink dress wraps her arms around the fat neck of a bald man with the build of a veteran wrestler; Nami can imagine the reek of sweat and cigarettes just by looking at him.

Nami orders a Pepsi-Cola, first time in his life. It costs as much as he earns in a day. As the girls disappear into the back rooms with the men, Nami is left by himself. He drinks the bottle of Pepsi slowly, through a straw, savouring its sweet deliciousness. He runs his hand over the chrome edge of the counter, while the reception clerk-cum-manager reads the sports page. Nami gets up and asks how much it costs to hire a girl. The man laughs and tells him the basic rates. Nami politely thanks him and thinks to himself, That's a lot. He puts on his cap and walks out.

Outside, a car squeals to a stop at the curb, and man with a cap on his head and a rucksack on his back leaps out and makes a run for it. The driver of the car gets out and chases after him. With the backpack bouncing heavily up and down on his back, the man is soon overtaken by the driver, who knocks him down and starts strangling him with one of the backpack straps. The two men struggle wordlessly for a minute, then the driver gets up, kicks the man, still lying on the ground, and goes back to his car. He starts the engine and quickly drives off. Nami bends over the fallen man and helps him sit up. The man sobs, bleeding from a gash on his face.

Back in the dormitory, Nami hurriedly masturbates, then tosses and turns a long time before being able to fall asleep.

***

Nami's workmate Nikitich teaches him that if you sketch a diamond shape onto the asphalt surface quickly enough, it barely leaves a trace. Practically the whole thing seeps into the base layer, which means you can only find it if you already know it's there. So the next time Nami is left by himself with the freshly laid asphalt, he furtively draws his pain into it; his gramma's large hands, the curves of a female body, the hens in the stinky henhouse, the three triangles. If he urinates on the drawings quickly, his secrets remain in the road surface, even if only in the form of blurred, illegible runes. One time the foreman catches Nami in the act and slaps him in the face, but he doesn't make him redo it. So Nami's secrets stay safely hidden away in the bumpy asphalt till the summer heatwaves and winter frosts crack them apart and they're crushed beneath the sulphur trucks' wheels.

With the whole sulphur complex asphalted through and through, and the entrance road as well, the only road still left is the one that runs from the warehouse to the lake and ends below water level. As Nami stands smoothing the asphalt over the road with his rake, it's a hot summer day. He's wearing thick work boots and greige pants covered with drops of tar, with his shirt tied around his head. Sweat runs down his naked chest. Nikitich sits in the shade, pouring water over his head from a plastic bottle, which he then tosses over his shoulder. Nikitich is a nice guy, about thirty-five years old, with a growing bald spot he covers up beneath a baseball cap. He likes to say he got his degree from the university of life. He reads newspapers and loves to philosophise. Given his spotted education, he often arrives at erroneous conclusions, but there's nobody to argue with him.

Nami looks up; the sky is blinding. To the west, he sees a dark cloud over the desert, and it's getting bigger and closer.

'Hey, Nikitich. What's that?'

Nikitich sits up and tips back his cap.

'Well, what the fuck is that?'

Nami, woozy-headed and sleepy, leans on his rake. The cloud is slowly coming closer and growing in size. Nikitich scratches his belly.

'Man, aren't those locusts?'

Nami begins to pick out individual dots in the cloud moving toward them.

'Holy cow! I've never seen that in my life! Have you?' Nikitich says with a childlike breathlessness. Nami shakes his head. He's never seen anything like it, though his gramma told him stories about how the locusts descended on Boros once and consumed every single thing growing on their little patch of land, all the food they had stored in reserve, even the schoolchildren's snacks and the radio cables! Nami can make out their bodies now, wings and outlines of black legs, as the locusts start descending to earth by the thousands. He has a dozen of them on top of him before he even realises it; he brushes them off hysterically. Most of them touch down on the still hot asphalt, where they get stuck and die far too slowly, chirring at unbearable volume.

'You monsters!' cries Nikitich. 'Fuck me! You screwed up my whole road!'

The locusts' bodies dry out and mummify in the heat, and the remains are left poking out of the asphalt surface till winter. The road looks like a five-hundred-metre-long carpet dreamed up by some wild designer; not a single car ever drives it. Only Nami goes for a stroll along the road every now and then, enjoying the strange melody of the dead insect bodies as they crunch beneath his soles.

***

Nami and the rest of the asphalt crew are reassigned to loading sulphur. Standing in the middle of a huge yellow field, they shovel clumps of sulphur mixed with fine, bright-yellow sand into wheelbarrows and push them to the slowly rising piles in two corners of the field.

'Hey, look, I'm at the seaside!' Nikitich shouts, lying on a sulphur dune. 'Just like vacationing on the Black Sea! Artek, pioneers! Sand as far as the eye can see! Check it out, Nami! You can get a suntan too! Just make sure you cover up that cute little nose of yours, so it doesn't get burned!'

Nami laughs. 'If the foreman comes, we'll be fucked.'

He lies down next to Nikitich and closes his eyes. It feels nice. The sun is still warm and he can hear the sound of water lapping against the shore even all the way from here. He rakes his hands through the sulphur sand and comes up with a big yellow crystal. He gazes through it at the sun, then thinks better and throws it away so Nikitich won't call him a fag. The other men are leaving for the day. All he can see of them is their sun-reddened backs coated in yellow dust. If they don't catch up to them, there won't be any water left in the showers when they get back. Nami is tired and lazy. He sits up and watches his departing workmates' backs. The sun is already hanging low, the horizon beyond the bay tinted red. The skeletons of the mining towers stand outlined against the sky, imposing extinct beasts, monsters seven stories high, their backs criss-crossed with shaky ladders. They stand atop the water's surface on platforms that, from time to time, in a fit of rage, the Lake Spirit pulls down to the bottom, but not today. Today the surface is calm and the evening inviting.

Nami feels a lump hit him in the leg. He looks around. Nikitich is staring straight ahead, but giggling to himself.

'What're you doing?'

'Who me? Nothing.'

And a moment later again, this time in the neck, just below his ear. Nami narrows his eyes; now Nikitich is openly laughing. Nami's heart starts pounding as he clenches his hands into fists. He rushes his workmate, but Nikitich is expecting it and knocks his feet out from under him. The two of them roll through the sulphurous sand, tumbling over and over each other, yellow crystals everywhere, even on their faces. Nikitich pokes at Nami, while Nami tries to grab hold of him around the waist. Nikitich is laughing like someone who's mentally deficient, totally at the end of his rope. He lies on his back in a heap of sulphur, laughing like a madman. Nami kneels on top of him, pressing his hands crossed against his chest. He can smell the odour of sweat, cigarettes, and sunflower seeds. He realises that he has an erection. He realises that the ugly-looking Nikitich is the first person who has physically touched him since the kolkhoz chairman.

'Jackass,' he says, climbing off and heading back to the showers.

The water is already all used up. The men are drying themselves off with dirty towels. The tiles on the floor are covered in a layer of yellow. Nikitich is still laughing as he steps into the showers. He pats Nami on the shoulder.

'C'mere, you jackass.'

He grabs Nami and gives him a hug. Nami stiffens but doesn't flinch. He stays a moment in Nikitich's arms, feeling the folds of his undershirt against his stomach. Tears rush to his eyes; he has to press his fist against his upper lip to stop it.

'Sonuvabitch, I could use a fuck,' Bald Kyril says from somewhere in the steam.

After that, nobody else says a word.

***

The next time Nami goes to the brothel, it's with Nikitich and another guy, who goes by the name of Kaktus.

'She's healing up. She got the clap,' the reception clerk says when Nami asks about the girl in the powder-pink dress. He's been saving up for her a long time, and now he's disappointed. He looks around to see if he can find a worthy replacement. But the other prostitutes seem lifeless, yellowed, and dusty compared to her. Nikitich has a brunette on his lap with broad Asiatic cheeks and a high, squeaky voice. Catching Nami's eye, he shrugs with a smile and gives the brunette a smack on the thigh.

'Here, have some,' the reception clerk says. He slides Nami a cutting board of sliced fatback that he's been working on as a consolation prize. Nami chews silently, arms pinned tensely against his sides, fingers clenched into fists.

'Why don't you go with Natasha then?' says the reception clerk after a minute or two. 'You'll have cosmonauts whizzin round your ears by the time she gets through teachin you.'

'Is she Russian?' Nami asks hesitantly. He's thinking about the catalogue of ladies' underwear.

'Of course, what else!' Nikitich laughs, tipping his head toward the corner where a chubby blonde of indeterminate age sits beneath a picture of a glittering landscape, legs crossed with both hands wrapped around her knee. The expression on her face is one of utter boredom. The reception clerk and the pimp nod to her in unison. She stands reluctantly and trudges to the counter. Colourful earrings shaped like a woman riding a white horse dangle from her ears. Nami can't take his eyes off her earrings, flitting like dragonflies over the water and sparkling in the same way.

Natasha chews, working her jaw, looking Nami straight in the eye. Nami shivers.

'Come on then,' she says. Without a word, Nami turns and follows her up the stairs. Nikitich watches closely, seeing him off with his eyes.

Natasha wears a vaguely coloured faux-satin dress. The slit in front is unravelling and there are threads hanging out. Peeking out from underneath is the shoulder strap of a pink bra. Her legs are nice and firm. The stairs groan in protest. So this is how it's going to be, Nami thinks. The first time he gets laid is going to be with a Russian whore he isn't even attracted to. The thought of it fills him with sadness.

The bedroom's so small that at first Nami thinks she mixed it up with the mop room. The door only opens halfway, since the bed is right behind it, and there's barely even enough space between the bed and the wall for Nami to stand.

'Leave them on,' Nami says, seeing Natasha go to remove her earrings. He leans against the wall and closes his eyes. Listens to the rustling of the satin. When he opens his eyes again, all Natasha has on is a pink bra and panties. Her thumbs are tucked under the straps on her shoulders, as if she wanted to take the weight off her shoulders for a moment. Her eyes are puffy and swollen. She looks like a fishmonger at the end of her shift. There's nothing sexy about her. Nami tries to focus in on the earrings, trying to think about Zaza. He closes his eyes and imagines the girls from the underwear catalogue. As he feels Natasha unzipping his pants, he squeezes his eyelids shut tight. He attempts an evasive manoeuvre, but Natasha takes a firm hold of his penis, refusing to be put off. Spitting into her palm, she curls her hand into a tube and slips it around his penis. The room's walls are painted green. Above the bed is a picture of a storm over a lake with a boat tossed by the waves.

Natasha's hand moves, slow and supple, warm between his legs. Nami opens his eyes and sees her staring absently toward the door, at a spot over the door frame where the plaster is crumbling. He has half a mind to tell her that she doesn't have to do this, if she wants to she can stop.

'I'm right here,' he says so abruptly it makes Natasha flinch. He grabs her chin and pulls her close. He touches her body, running his hand down her belly to her panties, then fingers a stiff scar running crosswise just over her pubic hair.

'Is that from a baby? Do you have a child?' Nami asks, realising he's excited.

Natasha nods without looking at him.

'Take off your clothes.'

Natasha, looking startled, quickly strips naked.

'How old is he?'

'Who?'

'Your child. How old is he?'

'Why?'

Nami fondles Natasha's heavy breasts, pressing up against her so hard that they both tip over and fall onto the bed.

'Ow!' Natasha hisses, clutching the back of her neck. 'What are you doing?'

Nami searchingly combs his fingers through the rings of light hair covering her pubic bone and thinks about the locusts sealed into the road. Natasha lies watching him with her head on the pillow. She shifts her pelvis toward him, but Nami presses his whole body up against hers, taking her in his arms and sucking at her breasts; the skin on her breasts is light and milky with blue-green veins shining through, and large pink nipples. Nami acts like he's lost his senses, squeezing and hugging Natasha, clinging to the worn-out Russian hooker like a drowning man, crying.

'There, there,' Natasha says, stroking his hair. 'What's the matter, little boy?' She turns onto her side and he curls into a ball in her arms.

Nami's body shakes with sobs. A huge reserve of something deep inside him has been hit, and now it's gushing out and there's no way to stop it. His cheeks are drenched. Even the grubby light-blue sheet and Natasha's breasts are soaked. She does her best to soothe him, humming to him softly until finally he gets tired and the flood of tears dries up.

Once Nami has calmed down again, Natasha tells him about her child. He's an eight-year-old boy named Vova and he has a vision impairment, but he's nice and round and has a lovely singing voice. He lives with Natasha's mother, who cares for him like the apple of her eye, much better than Natasha could manage on her own. Natasha can't stop smiling as she speaks about her boy, and Nami would like to tell her to be quiet, but he's too tired. He regrets the money he spent, thinking maybe he should have bought a Pepsi-Cola instead. In one short spasm, he presses up against Natasha and climaxes in tears.

'So how was your fuck?' Nikitich says, winking at him as they leave. He wearily lights a smoke.

'It sucked,' Nami says. 'She was lazy as an ox's legs in August.'

Nikitich nods meaningfully. 'I thought so.'

Once again, Nami steps out in front of the Symfonie

brothel. He stands at the entrance a moment, red and blue neon blinking frantically overhead, then turns and heads to the port. In an unwelcoming, overheated pub full of hostile-looking dirty men, he downs half a bottle of liquor. He feels something moving inside of him, like some ravenous animal that has awakened. On his way home he stumbles over a sleeping Ouroubor, and the beast in him is enraged. It spits and hisses, wanting Nami to show it something new, something besides the sordid watering holes, the dirty men and injustices. It wants to taste blood.

Nami kicks the sleeping man till blood spurts from his broken nose. The man groans, frightened and confused. Nami throws up, trying to disgorge the beast from his bowels.

***

The days flow by, lazily, haltingly, like the aphids on the plum tree outside the dormitory window. Nami shovels the sulphur into wheelbarrows, then pushes them to the conveyor belt that loads the sulphur onto the cargo ships. His muscles are massive and his palms hard as a grindstone. Each day he walks from work into the city, still covered in yellow dust, and walks the streets with a map in his hand, peeking into businesses and crossing them off as he goes. He spots his mother several times, and twice runs into Zaza, but it's never actually them. There are other people he also meets on his rounds more than once; he nods to them in greeting but doesn't talk to them. It would just be a waste of time, since he's only here temporarily. He's started having stomach pains, so he buys some goat's milk at the market and downs it on the spot. The pain doesn't ease up; the beast is digging a burrow inside him.

Evenings, the men in the dorm drink hard liquor and

play cards or backgammon. Nami is too exhausted to join them, so he watches from his bunk or else just falls asleep. Occasionally a brawl breaks out, and one night it ends in a stabbing, but nobody bothers to call the police or EMS. A big pool of blood is left behind on the floor. Nami turns his head to the other side and shuts his eyes. He can't stand the sight of blood.

'Hey, young one, clean that up.' Bald Kyril, a stocky guy who smokes foreign cigarettes and is involved in every brawl, rattles Nami's bed. Nami feels his heart jump, but he's too tired to climb down from the bunk.

'Kiss my ass,' he answers softly but clearly. The bald man hops up like a jack-in-the-box, manically waving his fist in the air, but Nikitich without a word stands from his pallet, blocking the way.

'The fuck you think you're doin, Nikitich?!'

'Leave him alone, Baldie,' Nikitich says.

Voice cracking, Bald Kyril screams, 'Fuck your gramma!' and slams his hands into Nikitich's chest. Nikitich grabs hold of his wrists and slaps Bald Kyril across the face with his own palms, *smack smack*!

'Keep fuckin with me and I'll wipe up that blood with your undies,' says Nikitich coolly, letting go of the man.

'I'll get you back,' Bald Kyril hisses through his teeth, and backs away.

'Thanks,' Nami tells Nikitich. He's exhausted, but it's still a long time before he can get to sleep. All night long the man who got stabbed keeps moaning. The blood on the floor dries to a shiny, crimson-black glaze that quickly peels away, and Nami's roommates are soon spreading it around the room on their soles.

***

On Sunday, Nikitich takes Nami to the amusement park. He buys him cotton candy and peanuts roasted in caramel. Squeezing themselves into the small, colourful bumper cars, the two of them sit there as awkwardly as monkeys at a wedding. Then, doing their best to look serious, they slam into each other so hard that Nami can feel his vertebrae pop. As soon as the cars come to a stop, Nami begs Nikitich to let them take one more ride. Nikitich laughs, wondering how it ever even crossed his mind to take Nami to a brothel, and when the attendants come around, they both stay sitting behind the tiny steering wheels and Nikitich pays for one more ride.

On the swing carousel Nami gets sick to his stomach, and the shooting gallery reveals that Nami can't shoot for beans—unlike Nikitich, who completed basic training in the motorised rifle division. Firing at a spinning target with a crude painting of a mermaid on it, Nikitich hits her nine times out of ten right in the heart. He wins the prize of a soccer ball with the paint already peeling, so it's obviously a reject, but that doesn't matter. Nami's so moved when his friend gives him the ball, he almost gives Nikitich a hug; he's never had a ball of his own.

After the shooting gallery, they go to the Ferris wheel, with its yellow-roofed cars, richly decorated with drawings of genitals, messages, and the names and phone numbers of previous visitors scratched into the paint inside. The wheel turns slowly. Nikitich and Nami are seated closely together inside the small space and the conversation lags.

'I'll sign our names at least,' Nikitich says finally, pulling a ballpoint pen from the pocket of his flannel shirt.

GLEB NIKITICH AND NAMI THE ORPHAN, UNIVERSITY OF LIFE, he writes among the other names in all capital letters. He examines his work with a look of satisfaction.

'University of Life. Good, right?'

'Nice writing,' Nami says with an approving nod, staring into the distance.

They're high up in the air now, nearly at the top of the ride. From this height he can see the whole city: the villa district, the glittering skyscrapers of the oil companies, the mining towers, and the long strings of oil tankers stretching beyond the horizon on the surface of the lake. Nami is overcome by a wave of dizziness. He takes a breath and holds it, and as his blood oxygen drops and the pulse in his head beats so strong he can hardly stand it, he clutches the soccer ball tightly in his lap, thinking about his own university of life; he can see almost the whole thing, laid out before him like it was on a plate.

'You said we'd be able to see Boros,' he finally blurts, gasping for breath.

Nikitich shrugs and pulls a pack of cigarettes from his pocket. It's windy up at the top, so it takes him a while to get one lit.

On their way out of the amusement park, they stop at a refreshment stand. Nikitich downs four large vodkas in a row, and on the way back he wraps his arm around Nami and tearfully tells him the story of his girlfriend, 'who I moved to the capital for, so with these hands here'—he waves his one free hand in front of Nami's face—'I could earn enough to buy us the house where she whored around with some guy who ran a garage.'

'Watch yourself with women, bud. It's a trap, and every decent guy falls for it! You'll see for yourself I'm right!'

Nami says nothing, running his tongue over some peanuts stuck between his teeth.

'It's a trap, you'll see!' Nikitich sobs, stroking Nami's face. He stumbles a few times, and each time Nami is there to catch him. It's dark out now, the streetlamps shining only sporadically.

'Come on!' Nami orders him. 'We got work to get up for tomorrow.'

Nikitich follows him like a sheep.

***

The sulphur is poured from the wheelbarrows onto a conveyor belt, which carries it up an incline and drops it into a hopper, an inverted cone the men call the Old Virgin. The lower part of the funnel is cut off, with a bottom that grates open and closed, discharging the jiggling sulphur crystals in a continuous flow.

Nami and Nikitich stand by the conveyor with their wooden rakes, watching to make sure too much sulphur doesn't fall off the cracked and punctured vulcanised rubber belts before reaching the hopper. Their faces are covered with primitive canvas respirators that have zero effect on how much sulphur dust they inhale. The rattling Old Virgin swallows up one wheelbarrow of sulphur after another, and spits it out onto the cargo ship, where another two men quickly rake it out of the way.

'Can you imagine doing this fuckin job the rest of your life?' Nami asks.

'Why not?' Nikitich laughs into his mask. 'You get to be out in the fresh air. You get to, uh ... There's no other advantage I can think of.'

'You're an ass,' Nami laughs.

'Whatever,' say Nikitich, leaning on his rake. 'Lunch'll be soon.'

Nami thinks that even if he had something to eat with him, he wouldn't be able to consume it for stomach pain. He tilts his head back, looking up at the sky swept clean of clouds. A swallow flies by low overhead, a tanker on the lake sounds its horn.

'Nikitich!'

Bald Kyril stands on shore underneath the conveyor belt, waving something over his head. It looks like a file or an envelope. Nikitich slowly turns his head and nods.

'I've got something for you!'

'What is it?'

'Guess! Maybe a letter from home. Maybe headquarters sendin your pay cheque. Or maybe it's those porn mags you ordered, right?'

'Fuck off, Baldie. I'll get it from you when I go to lunch.'

'Here, catch!'

'You dipshit, don't you dare.'

The envelope flies through the air, sailing in between Nami and Nikitich. Nikitich makes a grab for it but comes up empty-handed, loses his balance, staggers. Arms flailing, legs kicking, Nikitich slips and falls into the hopper after the envelope. Nami closes his eyes and tries to do the same with his ears. He hears a clunk from the bottom of the Old Virgin, then a grating, then the whole structure shakes and Nami hears Nikitich cry in disbelief, 'For the love of God, my hand is gone!'

Nikitich thrashes about, trying to wedge himself against the sides of the hopper using his left arm and legs. His right hand is gone from the wrist down. Nami stares at his workmate, unable to move, unable to shout, intestines turned to concrete. The blood-soaked gate at the bottom of the Old Virgin opens and closes menacingly as Nikitich struggles to keep his feet wedged against the wall. Nami numbly moves forward and leans over the edge to hand Nikitich his rake. Nikitich just rolls his eyes, as if trying to say he doesn't deserve such an idiot, but in fact he's losing consciousness. He gives up thrashing and lets himself slide down to the bottom, where the Old Virgin's timeworn but inexhaustible womb goes right on opening and closing.

'Baldie, turn it off!' Nami tries to shout, but all that comes out of his mouth is a wheeze.

He waves his rake over his head until finally someone notices and shuts down the machine.

The siren wails; it's lunchtime.

***

Nami never returns to the sulphur factory.

That evening, he waits for Kyril out in front of the workers' dorm, and when the bald man walks up, Nami lays into him with his fists. He is hopelessly inept and clumsy, fuelled by nothing but rage, having never had any experience in fights. Although drunk and caught off-guard, the bald man reacts automatically, by reflex–throwing a fist, he connects with Nami in the stomach, making him double over in pain. Nami groans, but then snaps right back up. Kyril lands another punch, this time on his right jaw. Nami keels over onto the ground. Kyril gives him a kick in the stomach and sits down astride him. Nami attempts to return his blows, but all he can make contact with is Kyril's sinewy belly. The two of them wordlessly pummel away at each other, their fists gradually moving slower and slower. 'A real fight is over almost before it begins,' Nami thinks, remembering what Nikitich used to say. It's embarrassing how long this is taking. He exerts whatever strength he has left to try to throw Kyril off, but the bald man is squatting on him like a truck full of rocks.

As Nami lies wheezing, Kyril finally rolls off. 'I hope you remember this lesson,' he pants. He gradually gets to his feet and bends over, hands on his knees, gasping for breath. Nami slowly stands and nods. 'You bet.' He throws a kick with his right foot to the bald man's face. Hears something crunch. Kyril topples to the ground, moaning. His face is covered in blood, or at least that's what it looks like to Nami in the dark.

Nami packs his things and vacates the dorm. The pain in his belly subsides, but his face is swollen for several days and he probably has a concussion as well.

***

A big black car, an off-road model but spotless, like it just left the showroom. The engine purrs like a well-fed kitten. It pulls onto the shoulder; a young man in an expensive suit sits behind the wheel, longish curly hair, shoes sparkling like water in the sun. He gets out of the vehicle and leaves the engine running; the cool fragrance of car freshener wafts from the interior. Two men from the first row of job seekers rush forward to polish the hood. The young man pays them no attention, making his way through the men lined up along the road. He pauses a moment to give Nami the once-over, lowering his head to look over the rims of his fancy sunglasses. He gestures to Nami with one hand to get in, climbs back in behind the wheel, and holding his nose with his fingers, he revs the engine and pulls out before Nami can even close the door.

The guy calls himself Johnny. He went to college in Texas and now works for an international oil company. Johnny knows how to drill wells and, most importantly, how to sell the oil that gushes from them. He needs someone to take care of his apartment and his personal affairs. Someone he can trust and who knows how to mind their business. Which is why he doesn't want a woman or anyone older than him. One thing for sure is, the first thing Nami needs to do is shower. The smell is unbearable. It just won't do. Johnny's voice is high-pitched and pleasant, almost feminine. Every so often he stops talking and rubs his nose. He doesn't ask

Nami any questions, not even whether or not he wants the job. It's a given. It's all been decided long in advance. Nami doesn't say a word as they cruise through the streets around the bazaar; with the windows closed and the air conditioning on, they can't smell the odour of rotting vegetables or the aroma of burek with sheep cheese. Nami doesn't say a word even as they pass through the better districts, with their marble exteriors and gilded front doors. He doesn't say a word as they drive past the Versace and Armani boutiques, the Irish pubs and Mexican restaurants for foreigners. The Hyatt Hotel and the glass and concrete offices of the global corporations rise menacingly into the sky like giant erections, as out of place as a man in a tuxedo at a cheap buffet.

The district where Johnny lives is calm and quiet. The streets are nearly deserted, not even a stray dog. They drive into an underground garage with rows of black, red, and lemon-yellow jeeps and limousines. Nami can hear the hum of air conditioning as he steps out of the car. At the far end of the garage, a hunched man pushes a sweeper over the concrete floor. Johnny is talking to someone on the phone. He's tall, with long limbs, and reminds Nami of a spider or a mosquito. Nami shuffles his feet. Johnny tips his head to indicate he should take the bags from the car, and Nami obediently grabs a few plastic bags and a melon, strawberries, eggs—all things he hasn't tasted in months. There's a cardboard box with several bottles of alcohol: vodka, gin, and rosé wine. Johnny is still on the phone as Nami follows him out of the garage, trying his best not to drop anything.

The elevator is quiet, silver from floor to ceiling, with a mirror on the inside. It's the first time Nami has seen himself in months and he's startled to discover he has two wrinkles between his eyebrows and a smudge of dirt on his cheek. If this is him, where is the boy from Boros? He frowns at himself, then closes his eyes. On the fifteenth floor, the elevator gently dings, and Johnny gestures to Nami with his head for him to get off. The apartment is spacious, with floor-to-ceiling windows, and thick carpets in earth colours. Hunting trophies adorn the wall.

Johnny disappears for a moment into the bedroom, with a huge bed surrounded by mirrored walls and a tiger-skin rug on the floor. When he comes back out, he shows Nami around the apartment: a terrace with exotic plants that need tending; refrigerator, washing machine, microwave, dryer. A blue-grey cat hisses at them from underneath the zebra-skin couch. Nami nods, Yes, of course, no big deal, he's seen it all before. He isn't some country bumpkin.

'Feed the cat, every morning, here's where I keep his food. Plus once a week you have to buy him chicken liver. Well, I'll be damned. Don't tell me you've never seen a shower? Really?'

Johnny rolls up his sleeves and shows Nami how it works. He ends up getting soaked, but he just laughs it off. Nami actually has seen a shower before, but only ones with the head so corroded that the water barely dripped out and only when the water was even running to begin with. A polished chrome beauty like this, with rain shower and massage settings, and the walls lined with malachite tiles that looked like they'd been stolen from under the noses of the warriors of the Golden Horde while they slept in the jade mountain of Kolos, now that was new to him. As far as Nami was concerned, all these expensive, luxurious things were just stupid and pointless.

'Here's the bathtub, it does massage too. Probably best if you stay out of it. Come on, I'll show you where you're gonna sleep.'

Nami starts in shock; it never entered his mind that he might be provided with a roof over his head. So he doesn't object when Johnny opens the door to a closet with a mattress on the floor and some portraits in old frames leaning against the wall. The mattress is used but in brand-new condition, and in any case Nami has never laid on a mattress before. He gingerly sits down on it with his knees to his chin. He can smell the stench of his clothes from weeks without washing. The mattress is soft and springy, so delicate compared to the ragged, flea-ridden straw mattress from the workers' dorm. It reminds him of a fairy tale his gramma used to tell him, about a poor young lad who winds up in the tsar's castle by accident.

'Unpack the groceries and wash up. You smell like a Russian tour group,' Johnny says. 'Then fix me something light for dinner. Next time you can do the shopping yourself.'

Nami nods. When he goes to the bathroom, he examines himself in the mirror; again, he has the feeling he's looking at a stranger, as if the director of a film had suddenly cast a new actor in the role of a character who develops over time. His body is more manly now, with honest-to-goodness trapezius and triceps muscles. His eyebrows and jaw are more prominent, and his chin has fine hairs growing in. There are ringlets of dark hair on his legs and chest–how did he not notice those before? He lathers up with lots of suds and combs his fingers through the hairs as the stream of precious hot water beats down on his body. He keeps expecting the water to run out, but he doesn't want to just walk away. Is it possible it could go on flowing like this forever? It seems like it will never end. Eventually Nami climbs out of the shower and slops across the emerald-green tiles, wet feet leaving behind a trail of suds. The mirror is fogged up. He wipes it clean and sees himself in fuzzy outline, definitely more man than boy; water drips from his hair. Nami likes the way this person looks but can't identify with him. There's something disturbing about the image in the mirror, something unfamiliar, something that draws him into the landscape beyond the mirror. He opens the door to the hallway and the steam comes billowing out. Nami stands buck naked in the doorway of the luxury bathroom, light at his back. Seeing he has an erection, he drapes a towel over it and tries to swing it back and forth.

Johnny stands in the bedroom doorway, smoking something that smells of vanilla and watching him with an amused look.

Nami quickly puts on the worn Adidas T-shirt and tracksuit that Johnny gave to him. He goes to the kitchen and opens the fridge, looking for something he knows how to prepare. Jars of caviar and apricot jam, a bunch of carrots, two cloves of garlic, a melon, a carton of strawberries, some still unopened Italian cheese, a smelly chicken liver, and champagne, lots of champagne. Butter and eggs. What's he supposed to do when he's never cooked in his life? He struggles awhile figuring out the glass-ceramic cooktop, then tosses a lump of butter in a pan and once it heats to a golden foam cracks in three eggs. As a final touch, he garnishes it with a chunk of gorgonzola and a spoonful of caviar.

'Dinner,' he calls to Johnny and shrugs. Johnny lies on his bed, rubbing his temples. The bed is so big you could land a helicopter on it. The cat lies at Johnny's feet, sizing Nami up with a hostile look. A drawer is cracked open in the nightstand next to the bed, and Nami spots a few small plastic bags and a gun. Johnny notices Nami's looking and nods. He gets up and goes to the kitchen. Picks up the plate of food, eyeing it suspiciously, sniffs at it, then dumps its contents into the garbage disposal. Nami swallows dryly as he hears the food going through the grinder.

'I lost my appetite,' Johnny says. He opens the freezer

and pulls out a bottle of vodka, then disappears with it back into the bedroom. Nami wordlessly washes the plate, dries it off, and puts it away in the cabinet. Then he sits down at the table and stares out the window. From the height of the fifteenth floor, he can see the stalls of the bazaar, the villa district, the port and the rippling waves on the surface of the lake, the tankers and mining towers in the distance. Outside the windows, the whistling monotone of the wind. Johnny is on the phone again, Nami can hear him raising his voice. He feels tired and sleepy. He switches on the wall TV, lays his head on the table, and falls asleep.

***

A few hours later, he's woken by voices. It's dark out now and the apartment is crowded with people. Two beefy men in leather jackets, one fragrant young gentleman, who looks as if he just stepped out of an ad for something extremely clean, and three young girls with long, glossy legs and lots of showy accessories, arguing over something in a whisper.

'Did you get a butler, Johnny?' laughs one of the girls, a brunette with her eyes a bit too far apart and silver hoops in her ears. She reaches across Nami's chest to take a bottle of champagne out of the refrigerator, squeezing unnecessarily close. Johnny leans on the kitchen counter, watching as she rubs her hips against Nami. Nami has to fight back the urge to touch her breast as it sways over his shoulder.

'Slow down, babe,' Johnny says calmly. The girl's face turns serious as she eyes Nami intently.

'Such a tender young boy,' she says sadly, stroking Nami's cheek.

'Hey, Diana, take it easy. Lay off the booze already.' Johnny laughs, pushing the girl into the bedroom ahead of him. Nami gets up and goes to lie down in his closet. He has a splitting headache. His eyes close the moment his head hits the pillow, and as he drifts off to sleep he hears the sound of frantic thrusting, the pitiless smack of flesh on flesh slapping like a sail in the wind. In a few minutes, the girl's moans turn to a continuous wail. A man's voice issues a single forceful atavistic groan, a primal scream, and then falls silent. Nami sleeps fitfully, but straight through till morning. When he wakes up, he opens the windows to air out the apartment, empties the ashtrays, gathers up the glasses, washes the dishes, and puts the cat out on the terrace.

One of the girls is asleep on the couch in the living room, gold dress hitched up around her waist. She has no underwear on. Nami stops a moment to take in the view of her spread shaved genitals; it reminds him of their cat Sana, shamelessly rolling around the stoop in Boros on a sunny afternoon. He stands there regarding the girl, scratching his left arm. Something tells him it's going to be a hot day today. The girl shifts position and Nami quickly tiptoes off to the kitchen. The girl lets out a soft snore and turns onto her side. For the rest of the day, Nami can't stop thinking about the terrifying nature of a woman's naked cunt.

***

The following days pass at a similar pace. Nami gets up in the morning and makes Johnny breakfast. Which Johnny typically leaves on the plate getting cold and only drinks coffee. Then smokes his first joint and leaves for work. Nami eats Johnny's cold breakfast, tidies up, washes the laundry, tends to the cat and the flowers on the terrace. Then he does the shopping and hangs around for the rest of the day. Occasionally he turns on the TV, but he mostly finds it boring. Sometimes he goes out for a walk; in which case he always stops by the park to talk to Majmun. The monkey may take an apple or wafer cookie from him, but he never shows any sign of finding Nami's presence enjoyable or that he even remembers him from before. He just creeps off into the corner and quietly eats his treat, exhibiting neither gratitude nor affection.

Johnny has generously invited Nami to go ahead and use the phone whenever he needs to, but Nami has no one to talk to. So instead he calls the shopping channels and erotic phone lines he sees on TV. After a chat with the operators, he no longer feels so alone, at least for a while.

Sometimes Johnny gives Nami a special errand to run, and he walks down to a street in the port to pick up a small package from a guy in a striped T-shirt who looks to him like a mummy. The man doesn't say anything, staring off into the space behind Nami. He literally never says a word. Nami thinks he's mute. He sticks the brown paper package into his pocket and goes to sit on the pier. Watches the big tankers sailing out, so loaded down their waterline is deep below the surface, and spits into the water. Every now and then he walks through the port to swim at the city beach. In his childhood days, the water ranged from turquoise blue to emerald green; the colour now resembles that of opalescent rotting mud. The water is so salty no fish can live in it. You can lie down on it like a blow-up mattress; your body barely breaks through the surface. Nami floats in the water, resting his head on the lake's salty pillow. Afterward, at home, he takes a long shower to get rid of the nasty itch. Once he breaks out in big red patches all over his body; after that, he stops going to swim in the lake for good.

He still walks the streets of the capital, peeking into bistros, game rooms, and smoky dives. Meeting his mother, he's convinced, is just a matter of being in the right place at the right time. He has no idea how or what his mother looks like, but he knows he has to make it happen. As he walks the early morning streets, seeing the still-sleeping homeless people, wrapped in cardboard boxes and clothes that are filthy and falling apart, he can feel the Spirit of the Lake already hovering over them.

For the most part they were Ouroubors, evicted from their homes years ago, when officials ordered several villages flooded to expand the lake. Unable to visit the graves of their loved ones, the normally peaceful Ouroubors began to rebel and set fire to Russian trucks and construction equipment. Allegedly the decision to liquidate them had come from the great Statesman himself; those who survived and now eked out a living on the capital's streets told of commandos in unmarked uniforms loading whole families and clans onto trucks, then shooting them out in the woods into pits that they themselves had to dig. It sounded far-fetched to Nami, like the legend of the sleeping warriors of the Golden Horde in Kolos Mountain. He saw the Ouroubors as fanciful unfortunates, but often engaged them in conversation, and every now and then he'd give one of them a loaf of bread or a hunk of ham or some vegetables on his way home from shopping for Johnny. The Ouroubors lived in tents and shelters made out of cardboard, and apart from the occasional public disturbance and drunken brawl, they were as harmless as a broken washtub.

***

Johnny often has company at home in the evening, whether a whole noisy crew or just Diana, the girl with the dark pageboy haircut, a gap between her upper teeth, and big hoops in her ears; that usually ends with the two of them having loud intercourse in the bedroom. Other times

Johnny doesn't come home in the evening at all, arriving by taxi at three or four in the morning, then dragging Nami out of bed wanting to talk, but there are times he crashes before he can even stagger into the bedroom; then Nami has to undress him and put him in bed and heat up some milk to make sure he won't throw up.

Nami doesn't get paid, but he's allowed to keep whatever money he has left over from the shopping and the errands, plus he has a roof over his head and food and Johnny's hand-me-down clothes. Not only that but Johnny has actual pornography, which the pages from the underwear catalogue can't compare to. As often as not, the magazines Johnny leaves for him are still untouched and sealed in their plastic wrapping. And for that matter, the voices from his bedroom are increasingly rare.

***

Nami is spellbound the first time he goes to visit Johnny in his office on the top floor of the high-rise owned by the multinational oil company that employs him. From wall to wall the floor is lined with bright-coloured carpeting, the walls are hung with paintings, and fragrant, well-dressed people converse with one another in a soft, polite tone of voice. Sitting behind the reception desk is a buxom blonde straight out of one of Johnny's porn magazines, and perched on every desk is a quietly humming computer. The shiny-chrome espresso machine in the kitchen trembles excitedly but refuses to give Nami his coffee. Even the telephones don't ring but instead buzz unobtrusively. Nami honestly feels as if he were in a dream.

***

The summer is exceptionally hot and the lake is evaporating even faster than ever. It's like it's gradually turning into a swamp.

Nami knows that Johnny keeps a gun or revolver in his bedside table, and never stops thinking about that fact. But when he sees Johnny standing in the doorway with a shotgun, it startles him so badly he trips over his words. Johnny gives a mischievous laugh. Nami sizes him up out of the corner of his eye, and seeing that he's sober and bathed, feels a bit relieved.

'Make me some coffee and then I'll tell you what we're going to do today,' Johnny says. Nami is a bit frightened at the suppressed excitement in his voice, as he is by the fact that Johnny has on a military uniform. The last time Nami experienced the combination of rifle and uniform was in Boros, and the memory still sometimes wakes him from his sleep with a painful start.

'I'll tell you what we're going to do today,' Johnny repeats.

They have a job, Johnny says, an assignment from the city itself. The esteemed officials of City Hall have chosen only the most dependable residents to carry out this assignment. Naturally, only those who have firearms and are experienced hunters. Of course they could ask the police or the army to deal with it, but that would fly in the face of tradition and professional honour. It is the responsibility of every upright man to prevent catastrophe, are we agreed? The more Johnny said, the more confused Nami was.

Within sight of the port, some six miles away, was an island that used to be home to a biological laboratory. Surely Nami had heard of it, yes? The lab was used to test biological weapons on animals, yes? Anthrax, plague, brulosis. Brulosis? Bruellosis? Brucellosis? Something like that. Meanwhile the Russians had long since abandoned the base and left the animals to their fate. According to occasional reports from the fishing boats that sailed past, a good number of the animals were doing well and had taken over the island. Dogs, sheep, rats, all lumped together. Now, with the lake's water level declining, there was a danger that the vermin would wade across to dry land and decimate the capital with diseases no one was prepared for.

Therefore every man with integrity and the ability to handle a firearm needed to do his duty. To do good. Johnny of course would walk in the front line and Nami would carry and load his guns, okay? And why was Nami so sweaty, for fuck's sake, was he really that hot? Nami shook his head. No, he wasn't hot. No, he wasn't going to load any fucking guns. Nami was going to stay home with the porn mags in Johnny's bed. But Johnny doesn't pay any attention. He's more hyped up at the thought of the slaughter than he is when he does coke. He tells Nami to make some meatballs for the trip, the guys'll get hungry for sure. They leave first thing in the morning, before dawn.

Nami stays up frying mutton balls long into the night. The sky in the east is smudged pink by the time he finishes, so there's no point in going to bed. He takes three bottles of vodka, thirty individually foil-wrapped meatballs, a loaf of bread, some onions, and a carton of cigarettes and puts them in a wicker basket. Then he sits and waits at the kitchen table, watching the eastern sky, mindlessly chewing on yesterday's bread, and once he finishes that, Nami has to settle for the nail on his own thumb. At three fifteen he gets up and goes to wake Johnny. But Johnny is already up, sitting on his bed, fastening on an ammunition wristband. He also has on a hunting vest with lots of pockets. He gives Nami an absent nod in greeting, but after the first cup of coffee he starts back in with the frenetic chatter again, trying to convince Nami what a patriotic duty it is they're going to perform and how grateful the nation will be.

They drive down to the port. Johnny parks the car and with the same manic energy relocates to the pier, where a bunch of other loyal patriots are waiting with the same idiotic vests and expressions on their faces. They stand around importantly, wielding hunting rifles and sports guns. One fool is even wearing a bandolier. Some of them look like they didn't sleep at all the night before, eyes bloodshot with the clouded look that drunkards tend to have. The men stand smoking in silence, occasionally broken by the sound of coughing or spitting. A few bottles of vodka circulate from hand to hand.

***

There are at least twelve boats. Nami can't even count them all. The wind is blowing so hard the waves have white caps.

'Gonna be some pukin out there,' the sailor on the boat carrying Nami and Johnny mutters into his beard. His name is Vaska. He sports a faded striped shirt and decades of experience at sea.

Johnny overhears and frowns. 'Do you even know what kind of mission this is?'

'Course I do,' says the seaman with a laugh. 'An important mission! How important? Very important!' He's in charge out on the water, so the rich-kid scum would do best to just sit back on the passenger bench and try not to vomit, Vaska says with his eyes. Nami smiles. The sailor has the same eyes as his grandad, and nobody screwed with him. Johnny frowns the whole rest of the forty-minute trip until the moment the island comes into view. Then his spirits suddenly lift again and his eyes shine with excitement.

They have one man-overboard incident along the way and several cases of severe nausea caused by large waves and previously ingested alcohol. This somewhat holds up the whole expedition, but shortly after daybreak they reach the island that once served as a home for biological experiments but has no name.

Nami tries in vain to keep from falling asleep, waking in pain each time his head drops to his chest. He's finally woken for good by Johnny's cry of amazement: 'Will you look at that shit? They're standin out here waitin for us!'

A herd of as yet unidentifiable animals stands on shore by the dock.

'Sheep?'

'Like hell! Those're dogs. Put on your glasses!'

'Looks to me like monkeys.'

'You boneheads are drunk as grape hoes.'

As Nami looks to shore, it soon becomes clear to everyone that the many-headed herd is in fact made up of monkeys, sheep, hens, and dogs. All the animals stand as one, expectantly awaiting the beloved people who so suddenly disappeared and have been so sorely missed. In the first row stand the dogs, a dozen, roughly, of various breeds, wagging their tails in excitement as they watch the boats arrive. Behind them, at a respectful distance, sit two monkeys of smaller stature, holding their penises. Then come the sheep with their typically stupid looks and a few smaller creatures that nobody can recognise from the water. None of the animals show any signs of disease.

'That can't be,' gasps Vaska under his breath. 'All those animals livin together here like they were in paradise. Wolf next to lamb. Well, bugger me.'

An orange and white spotted dog with long ears barks nervously. It eagerly dashes back and forth, toward the boats and back again. Finally it crosses the mud line: its paws sink down into the mud and it struggles to pull them out. Nami's heart pounds wildly. 'Run, you stupid ass,' he whispers.

'Hold your fire!' the retired general commands, but it's too late. Before the words are out of his mouth, the first shot rings out. It's surprisingly on target. The dog squeals and collapses into the mud. Nami can see its white fur soaking up the earthy colour of mud and blood combined. The dog's head gradually sinks lower and lower into the mire, till only its ears remain on the surface. A few pink-tinged bubbles come from its snout. Johnny, a graduate of Houston University and an employee of a multinational corporation, trembles with excitement next to Nami, biting his lip. Nami unintentionally glances down at Johnny's crotch, and seeing his erection, feels sick to his stomach.

***

Nami sits on the passenger bench, staring at the wooden box of ammunition in his lap. There are some letters stamped on the lid, but his vision is too clouded to make them out. Panic has broken out on shore. The dogs have lowered their tails and are looking to make themselves scarce as quickly as possible. The sheep bleat in unison, flocking en masse up a cliff overlooking the shore. The monkeys hug each other in terror. The men start jumping out of the boats and wading onto shore, cursing as they get stuck in the mud. They fire over each other's heads, seized with panic that the animals will escape before their rifles can get a word in. The retired general tries to issue orders, but is unable to make himself heard over the din.

'Just don't touch the beasts! Don't go anywhere near them, they're probably infected!'

No one hears or obeys. Meanwhile the sheep continue to stream toward the top of the cliff as if being pushed by a bulldozer. *'Meh meh meeeh,'* they cry, and it's hard not to hear in it the sound of a human lament.

'Enough!' Nami cries. No one pays any attention amid the deafening cannonade. Johnny left the boat long ago, not even noticing that his squire didn't follow.

The herd instinct meanwhile pushes the sheep further and further, the ones in front beginning to fall off the cliff into the mud below. They land with a loud smack. Many of the sheep break their legs and then can't lift them out of the mud, which makes them squeal all the more urgently. The ones that, by some miracle, manage to unstick themselves, are an instant later driven in still deeper as their flockmates plunge down on top of them.

The two monkeys, who opted to negotiate, are first to suffer the consequences—the fact that they didn't attempt to escape marks them for immediate death. All that remains on the spot where they were hugging a moment earlier is a mush of blood and fur. Nami, eyelids squeezed tightly shut, huddles in the boat. Vaska smokes in silence. The phalanx of men advances across the island, leaving behind a trail of mud and gore. Every now and then, a red burst of blood explodes like a flashing window sign amid the retreating herd of animals. Trailing behind the armed men is a group of volunteers from the civil defence in black jumpsuits with masks on their faces. They collect the dead animals in big black bags to be cremated later in large furnaces.

'I hope they all get anthrax,' Vaska says as a group of shooters disappears over the hill. 'I'm sure as hell not givin them first aid.'

The foresight of his remark becomes clear a moment later: the silhouettes of two men appear in the morning sun, carrying the body of a third across the bloodied plain. They drag him through the mud to the nearest ship, shouting to the captain to fire up the engine and radio for an ambulance to the port. Even at a distance of ten metres,

Nami can see the man has a bloody wound on his flank and his head turned to the side. His eyes are clouded over like they were on the sheep when Nami's grampa used to cut their throats: after their initial resistance, the determination to fight drained out of them, along with their blood, gradually giving way to a peaceful resignation. Nami realises that they wouldn't bring a shot man onto the ship alive. But he finds no satisfaction in it, only rage.

'That guy's dead,' Vaska remarks, and Nami nods in agreement. The boat with the dead man slowly sets out on its trip back to the capital.

'Aren't they gonna give him to the Lake Spirit?' Nami asks, tugging at his lower lip.

'They don't do that, son,' says Vaska, spitting into the water. 'They'll take him to the city morgue, then hold a funeral and dig him a hole in the graveyard. Womenfolk'll wail and act like they're gonna jump into the grave after him, but don't worry, they don't really mean it.'

'But that'll make the Spirit angry,' Nami says with a baffled look on his face.

'You bet it will,' the sailor laughs with a shrug. 'Hey, looks like our Golden Horde has returned.'

The hunters are trickling back from the other side of the hill. The first three are talking loudly, but the others walk in silence, alone or in twos. The sun is fairly high now, it must be around ten. It's starting to get hot and the men in the hunting vests are sweating. Some of them are stained with blood; one thin young man with no eyelashes has vomit on his pants. The sanitary brigade carries out a systematic cleaning of the coastline, so apart from the sheep buried in the mud there are no carcasses in sight. The retired general waits until everyone arrives, puffing away at a slim cigar. Meanwhile as the news of the lost life spreads, the men slip a little bit deeper into their sadness. The retired general calls them to attention and asks for a minute of silence. The men doff their caps and meaningfully clear their throats.

'You who are assembled here in this unit: operation completed, losses within acceptable limits! Gentlemen, I commend you! At ease!'

***

Nami has been following Johnny's spidery frame for a while now as he wobbles along the shore, searching for Nami among the men. The excitement has drained out of him, and his shoulders droop wearily forward, accentuating once again his sticklike, unathletic build. His curly hair hangs limply down from his peaked army cap, and his face is bathed in sweat.

'Nami!' he finally shouts. 'Nami, where the fuck are you?!'

Nami breathes a sigh, puts down the box of ammunition, and squeezes the food basket tightly between his calves. He stands up and jumps off the boat. Lands in water up to his chest. He wades along the boat to the bow, where Vaska hands him the basket, which Nami then carries through the mud, holding it over his head. It's not easy going; his feet sink into the mud with a sucking sound at every step he takes. It reminds Nami of the fairy tale about the giant beet. The mud smells awful. If his loved ones–his gramma and grampa–are here in the lake with him, they aren't giving any sign. To be lying on a towel on the city pier right now, watching the sun glint off the surface. There was nothing else he wanted more.

'Where were you?! Where the hell were you, you little shit?' Johnny lets fly the moment he catches sight of him wading through the mud. Nami wordlessly clenches his jaw.

'Why weren't you there by my side when the going got

tough, you filthy hick? When my life was on the line? I feed you, I clothe you–and you betray me like this?!'

He stalks through the mud to Nami, and once he gets close enough he shoves him in the chest so hard that Nami loses his balance and staggers. He tips over backward, and unable to dislodge the foot behind him from the mud, he plops onto his back, though managing to hold on to the basket, which now rests on his chest. The men burst out laughing.

'Our snack is here,' laughs Johnny triumphantly, raising the basket over his head. 'The two of us will settle this later,' he says to Nami through his teeth.

'No,' says Nami, awkwardly getting to his feet. The back of his pants are covered in stinking mud, and the situation in general doesn't offer him much hope of coming out of it with dignity. 'No, we'll settle it now.'

Johnny looks back in surprise, but Nami is already running at him and ramming his shoulder into Johnny as hard as he can. Johnny groans and sprawls flat out into the mud. With his rifle still in one hand and the basket of food in the other, he has no way to soften the fall. He lands with a loud splat, sending up a spray of mud. His whole body is splayed flat out: the peaked cap rolls off his head, his beautiful curls glued together with opalescent brown muck. The foil-wrapped mutton balls roll across the mud's surface like mercury beads from a broken thermometer.

A forgotten duck flaps out of the reeds with a cry. One of the hunters hefts his rifle and matter-of-factly shoots it down. The bird hits the water with a soft splash nearby.

Johnny gets to his feet with effort, face crooked, jaws knocked out of alignment.

'I'll give you a head start,' he hisses through his teeth. 'I'm gonna count to ten and then I start shooting.'

Johnny reaches for his ammunition belt and starts loading

his rifle. Counting, he's counting too fast. By the time Nami gets ashore, he's already at seven. Nami runs for all he's worth, he knows this is for real. His feet, weighted down with mud, are slowing him down. The thick layer of sludge covering his shoes makes it feel like he's got watermelons on the end of his legs. When he hears 'nine', he starts zigzagging. Johnny fires off two rounds. Nami counts ten and starts running straight while Johnny reloads and fires again. Nami goes back to zigzagging as he hears the other men merrily cheering Johnny on. After six shots, Nami reaches the crest of the hill, giving Johnny his last chance.

He hears the bullet whistle past and bury itself in the dirt, making a crater big enough to fit his hand in. Letting out a cry of disbelief, Nami drops to the ground and rolls over the back of the hill. He breathes quickly and shallowly, panting like a dog. He's not getting enough oxygen. He wraps his hands around his throat and looks into the sky. Watching the fleecy clouds drifting tranquilly by overhead, he soon calms down enough to catch his breath. He cautiously peeks out from behind a patch of dry alyssum and confirms that Johnny's not coming after him. Leaning on his rifle, with his hand to his ear, he's probably on the phone.

***

Nami lies for a long time curled up on his side, watching the clouds and feeling the mud on his body dry and harden. He hears the engines start up on the boats taking the heroes back to the city. And at last he's alone: Robinson on an island with no animals or trees, infested with diseases whose name he can't even pronounce. The realisation makes him dizzy: he forbids himself to think about it.

He gets up and climbs to the top of the hill. The island isn't large, measuring no more than a kilometre end to end at its longest point, extending northwest to southeast. The southeast corner, where the killing brigade had been anchored and there used to be a small dock, is now completely abandoned. On the other side of the island, however, Nami is surprised to find the sanitary unit still at work in their black hygienic jumpsuits. They move at a dreamlike pace, like burying beetles. Clearly it was an exhausting shift.

A short way from the dock stands the grey concrete building of the laboratory. On the flagpole in front, a shredded flag, its original colours now beyond recognition, hangs at half-mast. There are almost no windows or doors left on the building, the few that remain swing idly on their hinges. Nami sees a creeper vine that managed to find a way into the building through the window but withered and died mid-effort. The front door is sturdy, but half-buried in drifts of wind-blown dirt. Written above it in red letters is a notice:

WARNING
YOU ARE ENTERING A TOP-LEVEL BIOLOGICAL HAZARD ZONE
TAKE ALL SAFETY PRECAUTIONS!!!

The safety instructions are posted just inside the door in a cracked glass case. Dozens of animal tracks crisscross the dust on the floor inside. Apart from that, all he notices is a few cookie boxes and an empty can of condensed milk. Over each door in the hallway is a warning light encased in a plastic cover, at one time clearly red, though by now broken beyond repair. A bumblebee comes buzzing loudly down the hallway and flies out the door behind him.

In several of the rooms there are cages and terrariums, some of them still locked. Plainly their inhabitants met their death in them, but thanks to Mother Nature not a shard of bone remains. The only things left in the lab are those too heavy to have been taken away—stainless-steel tables, plexiglass hoods sans plexiglass, and metal cabinets and display cases with broken glass. Broken glassware crunches under Nami's feet.

Nami liked lab work when he was in school. He enjoyed handling the pipettes and test tubes. It made him feel like he was doing work like the people who were truly smart and sophisticated. Not in Boros, of course, but surely in the capital there must be people with white coats and sterilized hands. Even after going through all the drawers and filing cabinets, he doesn't find a single usable thing. A torn poster with bent corners hangs on the wall. Nami knows it well: the Statesman and his Eight Rules for the New Man. It dawns on him that this is the most dangerous thing in the whole lab. He pulls out a metal drawer and hurls it at the poster.

'Motherfucker!' he yells. He likes the sound of it, so he says it again, this time more calmly and with a touch of pathos, the way he used to recite poems about the benevolent Statesman in school. The look in the Statesman's eyes is sad, almost tearful.

In the room that served as the changing room, Nami finds no clothes except for a long white dress in one of the lockers. At first he thinks it's a lab coat, but looking closer he sees it's a ladies' dress made of light synthetic fabric, with flounces at the hem and gold-trimmed ruffles. Even greyed with dust, there can be no doubt: it's a wedding dress. All the girls from Boros got married in dresses like this one, except on their heads they wore a high cone-shaped cap, decorated with embroidery and a crest. Who on this island of despair was thinking of marriage so tangibly that they bought themselves a wedding dress? Nami leans his forehead against the open locker door and runs his fingers over the ruffles on the sleeve. The synthetic fabric grates unpleasantly against his skin, but he can feel the bride's hand behind the ruffles, smooth, slightly downy, and trembling with expectation. Nami tries to bring to mind the face of the girl, but he can't, she has no face. He can only smell the faint odour of mothballs and stirred-up dust.

There's no running water in any of the rooms. Nami opens his hands and looks at his palms: they're dirty and bloody and shaking. He can smell his own stink. Out in front of the building he finds a pump, and after a few rusty belches a thin stream of brown water issues from the spout. He can hardly believe his own luck after such a crazy day. He pumps like a madman, laughing away. He knows the water is just as toxic as the water in the lake, but it looks clean at least. He takes off his clothes and washes off his entire body, with difficulty but still. Then lies down naked in the sun. He's so thirsty. He falls asleep.

***

As the sun drops toward the horizon, Nami is woken by the cold. His skin itches and the tongue in his mouth is stiff and rough like pumice. Next impression: the short, intermittent honking of a boat horn. A fishing boat cruises slowly by the dock, similar to the one he came here on. Yes, it even has a similar name: *Vera*. And standing behind the helm is Vaska, who brought him here this morning, casually waving hello.

Nami quickly gathers up all his things and races down to the dock, waving wildly at the sailor.

'Yeah yeah, I see you,' Vaska says without a smile. 'I came back for you, boy.'

'Really?' Nami pulls up, one foot draped over the boat rail. 'You came back for me?'

The sailor pats him lightly on the back.

'Just don't get all emotional on me. And get yourself into some clean clothes.'

Nami offers a laugh out of courtesy, short and bitter. As they slowly leave the island behind, it looks almost bucolic in the glow of the setting sun. Nami wonders if maybe it was all just a dream.

'Half of those boneheads are from the police,' the sailor says. 'Two judges, the deputy mayor. The rest of em are just gutless scum who even the army wouldn't take. But you got nowhere to go to complain, buddy. You're gonna have to watch out for em now. Hell's bells, I got some spare clothes down in the cabin. Hop in there and have a look.'

Nami finds a fisherman's smock and waxed canvas overalls. They both smell of diesel, which Nami finds reassuring. It's a clean, industrial smell. The pants keep falling down, so he ties a rope around his waist.

He sits down on a heap of fishing nets at the bow and watches as the boat bumps over the waves. He doesn't even want to think about his situation. But one thing is clear: that sailor who rescued him is the Spirit of the Lake in one of its many guises.

Vaska leans against the wheel, cutting the engine to half throttle, just sputtering along. He manoeuvres the boat with an expert hand, but still has to be careful so the propellor doesn't get tangled in the algae overgrowing the lake.

'Attention to starboard!' Nami shouts, and the sailor nods, yeah, he sees it. They float past a sheep carcass: its coat the colour of mud, legs sticking up in the air. It looks as if it's smiling. Eyes open wide. Vaska coughs violently, the cough of a long-time smoker.

'If there really was somethin wrong with those sheep, now the whole lake's contaminated, thanks to those pricks,' he spits, giving the engine some gas. *Vera* leaps forward, raring to go.

'Know where I'm takin you?'

Nami shakes his head.

'It's your lucky day, boy. I'm takin you to the Old Dame's. In fact she's expectin you. I sent her a message through one of my friends who does maintenance over at her place. He told her all about you—how you knocked that sucker into the mud and dodged his bullets. Now she wants to meet you.'

'Who's the Old Dame?' Nami asks.

Vaska just shakes his head and spits.

***

The Old Dame used to be nobility. She lives behind an ivy-covered fence in one of the former high-class bourgeois villas, with the owners' initials falling off the crumbling facades, gardens with wild apple, almond, pomegranate and fig trees, and the withered hulls of hollyhocks. Today most of the villas stand next to some botched tenement building, an exit ramp, or a shopping centre with a worn-away facade. But they harken back to the wealthy times when oil barons were born by someone digging into the ground at random and hitting oil, spraying a geyser five metres high in the air, which then took several days to get under control. And one of these barons was the father of the Old Dame, the youngest of three daughters, raised by an English governess and educated in Paris, the centrepiece of every social event in the city and the catch dreamed of by every young man who wanted to make his mark in life.

Now the Old Dame's face is wrinkled like a crumpled sheet of paper. Unlike most women's voices, which age into an annoying falsetto, hers coarsened and dropped down somewhere into the tenor range: listening to her, Nami felt as if he were bathing in a subterranean river. Her swollen-jointed long fingers were adorned with gold rings set with large precious stones. Every week a hairdresser came to her home to tend to her hair. And every day except Sunday, the

Old Dame would play piano after breakfast for a half-hour; then she would write letters. On Sundays she went to the cemetery, where she visited the graves of her parents and both her older sisters. Though she may have been an old maid, no one believed the Old Dame was literally a virgin. She had seen her fiancé off to war; for a while he wrote back to her and then he stopped. She mourned for months afterward. When she finally promised her late beloved she would never marry, she found it greatly eased her grief. She then had a series of romances with prominent men, including the Statesman himself, who had stayed in the city for several years at the start of his career.

All of the city's notables came to her salon. Everyone who had ever meant anything had leaned against her dark green brocade wallpaper, tapping the ash from their strong Turkish cigarettes into the bronze lion's-mouth ashtrays, complaining about his lot. The Old Dame listened to them, either nodding along sympathetically or suggesting they stop whining and pull themselves together. In this house—as in several others—the city's shadow administration met; alternative threads of human destiny were spun here, collective solutions sought to desperate predicaments. It also saw the creation of an informal foundation for girls in delicate situations and orphans.

It is into one of these salons that Nami steps, filthy and exhausted, in a work jumpsuit tied round with rope, that evening when the fishing boat brings him to the capital. Most of the company is dressed in black. A cloud of white smoke hangs over the room, and the record playing on the turntable is a tango where a woman with a worn-out voice sings how it bleeds her heart out every night when her lover goes home to his wife. A violin and piano wail in accompaniment. It is the first time in Nami's life that he hears the sound of a scratched record skipping.

The moment Nami lays eyes on her, he can tell right away that she's the head of the household: her gaze is kind but piercing, her back straight but her movements relaxed and confident, albeit somewhat restricted by arthritis. She has a distinctive nose and droopy eyelids and is wearing a black lace dress with a pearl brooch pinned to her chest.

'Come here, darling,' she tells him, giving him a stroke on the cheek. Her hand is dry and hot, with a caress like sandpaper. It reminds him of his gramma, and he rubs up against it like a cat. As she leaves her hand resting on his cheek, Nami squeezes it between his chin and his shoulder. The Old Dame smiles in surprise and basks with him in a shared moment of private understanding before pulling her hand away. It smells of tobacco.

'Nice music,' Nami says, and she bursts into a fit of coughing laughter.

'You're right. Sentimental, kitschy, but nice.'

Nami is silent, not knowing what to say. He has no idea what either sentiment or kitsch are.

'Are you hungry?'

He nods.

The Old Dame beckons to the woman in the lace dress, who leans over to her.

'Hot milk for the boy, Vera. And throw in a shot of Georgian cognac. Oh, and heat him up some consommé.'

Vera gives him a disapproving glance but brings him a glass of hot milk so rich it makes his head spin. It turns out consommé is just ordinary broth with tiny liver dumplings and mini pieces of carrot floating in it, but it tastes wonderful and Nami asks for seconds.

'You're a brave boy, my dear. You deserve a medal, but in this strange time idiocy is valued more than heroism. In any case, you must know that there are still people able to appreciate it. Am I right, *mes amis*?'

Half a dozen people gathered around them smile. One madame, with feathers around her neck, starts to clap hysterically. The Old Dame cautions her not to drink anymore.

'To your health, my friend!' says a small, dumpy man—a woman's doctor who, as Nami later learns, has delivered a quarter of the capital—and raises his glass.

Nami awkwardly clears his throat. 'I think there may have been some misunderstanding,' he says quietly. He isn't certain if there are actually any sounds coming out of him, but it seems like everyone is listening to him. 'It was nothing pretty, just a fight in the mud. No heroism involved.'

'Revolutions have been ignited by smaller sparks,' the hysterical lady shouts.

'Please, make her some coffee. Martha, stop drinking, or I will show you the door,' says the Old Dame. The hysterical lady staggers.

'Revolution?' says Nami.

'Pff!' the Old Dame waves dismissively. 'Some revolution! Martha's just talking nonsense. If you take a bath, you can stay here tonight. After that we'll see.'

Vera appears displeased, but beckons to Nami, who summons up all his strength and follows her up the stairs. As his head reels, Vera's large rear end blurs into a huge splotch that covers up the entire world. She shows him to the bathroom, complete with flowered tiles, brass fittings, and a tub on bronze feet. Most of the taps have a drip, and some are coated with calcium deposits and rust. The bathroom has a scent of mint and early summer flowers, which Nami hasn't smelled in years. Vera fills the bath half full, with a decent amount of suds. Nami blissfully submerges himself, and remains that way, totally still, without even noticing that the water is getting cold. At last he falls asleep.

***

The next morning the Old Dame herself comes to his room with a glass of almond milk. She sits down next to him on the bed and just watches him, smiling, as he drinks. She rests her warm palm on his hand and Nami closes his eyes. As the sun shines through the window onto his bed, for a moment he allows himself the illusion of feeling safe and carefree.

Then the Old Dame goes downstairs to the drawing room, where she plays the piano.

***

For the next two days, Nami lies in bed not moving, not eating, and sleeping miserably. He thinks about his first time at the barber. The first time he scored a goal and smashed one of his ribs against the goalpost he was so overjoyed. The first time he almost drowned while he was learning to swim. The first time he drove a tractor. The first time he steered his grampa's boat. The first time he caught a firefly and Grampa stuck it to his forehead. He thinks about stupid things, the Peace Day celebration and the Russian commanders in their faded uniforms. About the silver fish tossing in the net. Everything that happened before. Before Grampa drowned, before the Lake Spirit took Gramma, the Russian savage Zaza, and the Old Virgin Nikitich's hand. He weeps without tears.

On the third day the Old Dame comes to his room with a stern look on her face. 'Enough whining,' she says. 'Get up, I need you to do some work in the garden.'

Nami doesn't say a word. The idea of garden work, or basically anything else he could ever imagine doing again, seems unimportant, useless, meaningless. He stares at the

Old Dame blankly. 'There's no point,' he finally says. 'I don't feel like it.'

'You don't feel like it? What if the guardsmen came right now to take you away to prison? Would you lie here like a bitch and sob?'

'What guardsmen?'

'What guardsmen, you ask? The ones you always have to be prepared for. Or the desperate man who hasn't eaten in a week, so he's determined to do whatever it takes, and all of a sudden you run into him in your own kitchen. The betrayal of friends who denounce you for fabricated crimes against the state. You have to be prepared to flee or fight at any moment, boy. Can't do that in bed, can you?'

'What guardsmen?' Nami repeats stubbornly.

'Well, I suppose you've heard that I was the Statesman's mistress. Yes? That was still in the days before he became the Statesman. He was already ambitious, but still handsome and full of youthful enthusiasm. I was very young and flattered by his interest. Well, yes, I did fall in love with him. I was hardly the first one it happened to!' she says, raising her voice.

She pauses, looking out the window into the garden. Then waves her hand.

'I'm sure it's happened to you too. There, on the shelf. Hand me that book with the red spine. Yes, the *National Fairy Tales*.'

Nami hands her the book and snuggles back under the covers. The Old Dame holds the book on her lap for a moment, then runs a bony hand over the dark-red leather binding and opens it. A little dust kicks up and whirls above the bed. The Old Dame leafs through the book; when she comes to the legend of the Golden Horde, she hesitates, turns the page, and there, lying next to a magnificent colour illustration of heroes on horseback in gold-quilted jackets and pointed caps, is a small black-and-white photograph. The Old Dame gazes at it for a moment, then hands it to Nami. It shows a tall, handsome man with slicked-back hair, a skinny tie, and a tentative boyish gaze. Standing at his side is a girl in lacquered shoes and a pleated skirt down to her knees. She leans against the man, chin stuck out, smiling cheekily into the lens, hand on her hip. Her dark-coloured hair is a little bit blurred. Probably at the moment the shot was taken, she moved her head or the wind blew. In the background, there are some coniferous trees and a dirt road with a donkey walking along it.

'You were beautiful,' Nami says in an obligatory tone and hands the photo back.

'Thank you. But politically undesirable,' the Old Dame smiles. 'One evening the two of us were planning a trip to Paris together, and the next day a brigade of semi-literate muzhiks broke down my door and confiscated all of his photographs and letters. Luckily this one I had well hidden. The third day I myself had to hide, first under the bed, then after that with friends, since my existence was too compromising for the Statesman. Well, of course he wanted to get rid of me. Are you surprised at that?'

Nami sits on the bed, leaning his back on the headboard, squeezing the corners of the blanket in his fists. He isn't surprised; he isn't really paying much attention to the Old Dame. Instead he's watching the morning sunlight as it pierces the blinds, casting shadows on the wall that dance before his eyes.

'Do you think if I had allowed myself to grieve like that at the time, that I would have survived?'

Nami gives an indifferent shrug.

'He went off to party headquarters and his career took off like a rocket. He married some ugly matron from the central committee with an impeccable political background and whored around his whole life with ballet dancers, singers, and figure skaters. You think that I wasn't crushed? That I didn't feel like my lungs were filled with desert sand? Like he'd buried me alive? I never heard another word from him again in my life. At least after that he stopped hounding me, and ultimately he died, so now I have peace.'

The Old Dame finishes speaking and coughs hoarsely. She slips the photo back into the volume of fairy tales and returns the book to the shelf. She carefully smooths her skirt and stands to leave the room. In the doorway she stops and looks back.

'So, Nami. Get your ass out of bed, change your clothes, eat something, and get to work. After that, we can discuss the matter of your mother.'

***

Nami sets to work in the Old Dame's garden, trying to make it look again like it did in the old photographs. He tears up shrubs, uproots weeds, lays down and fertilizes flower beds, to be planted with flowers and herbs in the spring, and prunes the trees. The watering is the hard part, since the district only has water in the mornings and the evenings, and it's prohibited to use it on the garden.

Evenings, a wide assortment of urban intellectuals, second-rate dissidents, and theatre prodigies from the last century come to the salon and engage in toothless debate about politics and the untenable state of society. Nami usually falls asleep in the armchair he has appropriated in his role as cat, and the Old Dame lets him have his way. Every morning she comes to his room with almond milk or lemon juice with honey and asks how he slept. Her eyebrows are smoothly plucked and full like those of a young woman. Then she goes down to the drawing room to play the piano and Nami listens. It was like time turned to stone in that room; dust floating noiselessly through the air, settling onto the plush furniture and brocade throws, the cabinets giving off the scent of naphthalene and sandalwood.

***

Nami gets up in the morning, has something to eat (he is constantly famished, devouring whatever he can find: a kilo of peaches from the basket in the pantry, a loaf of white bread, a hunk of cheese from the water bowl under the stairs, and a plate of couscous with cherry dressing), and goes out to the garden. Prunes the trees and cultivates the hollyhocks. He is sweaty, filthy, injures himself several times, and his ankles are covered in bruises, but he actually seems to enjoy it. He works to the point of exhaustion. When he comes back into the house, the Old Dame is wearing white gloves and a boa and is on her way out to the theatre, so they put off their conversation about his mother for now.

Then one day Nami announces: 'I rescued a rose from the weeds today. I almost didn't notice it and dug it up with the mugwort.'

'Oh yes? Next to the gazebo?' the Old Dame asks. For the first time since Nami has met her, she looks slightly upset.

He nods.

'Be sure to tell me when it blooms. I have to hurry off now.'

For the next few days, neither one of them mentions Nami's mother; Nami works intensively on building up new calluses while the Old Dame abstractedly sorts through her wardrobe. Vera runs back and forth, like a bewildered dog, between the Old Dame, Nami, and the mink furs and wool coats hung up in the courtyard, complaining that nobody ever tells her anything.

Nami doesn't ask questions. It's one thing making a vague resolution to search for your mother and another to know the truth lies waiting behind the nearest curtain; you just have to tear it down. Nami functions on autopilot, counting to himself softly while he works or reciting patriotic poems he learned in school. By the end of the day he's so miserable that it's obvious he's not in a state to talk, and after a short bath he just passes out straight into bed. The Old Dame acts as if she never even mentioned the word *mother,* but it turns out she was just gathering information.

Nami loses track of what year it is and how long he's actually lived in the capital. But the morning when the Old Dame walks into his room in a blue taffeta dress and sits down on the edge of his bed with a mug of warm milk, he knows for sure that it's early September and so his birthday will be in a month.

'Of course I know who your mother is,' the Old Dame suddenly lets drop as if she were following up on a previous conversation. Nami feels like pulling the blanket over his head. The shadows on the wall from the blinds are much more blurry now and moving faster.

'You're seventeen, aren't you?'

He shrugs. 'I guess. Yeah, probably.'

'Well, there aren't that many girls who came to the capital eighteen years ago from Boros, pregnant and too scared even to talk.'

Nami picks up the mug of milk and knocks it back without a word.

'Your mother's name is Marie Anna.'

The Old Dame pauses to see what effect it has on Nami. He acts as if he hasn't heard.

'She came here on the night train after some jerk in Boros raped her.'

Nami remains quiet, staring at the bottom of his empty mug of milk.

'He was a simpleminded village boy. Saw a pretty girl, the urge came over him, and he just ... jumped her. It didn't go too well for him when word got round of what he'd done. The what do you call it? Spirit of the Lake? Well, apparently it took the boy.'

Nami is silent.

'When Marie Anna got here, she was in such a state of shock she didn't talk to anyone. She was taken in by the family of the doctor who comes to see me and lived with them in return for helping out around the house. After a couple of weeks she found out she was pregnant. The doctor delivered her child–that would be you–then took him to stay with his grandparents in Boros.'

Nami sits impassively, though after a moment he nods.

'Listen, it's not that bad. There are hundreds of cases like yours. A lot of newborn babies just end up in the lake. You actually ended up all right.'

'So how do you know it was my mother?' Nami comes back at her. 'My mother would never let herself be raped by the village idiot.'

The Old Dame is silent.

'Besides, I've never heard any story like that in Boros!' Nami says, raising his voice. 'Never! That's ridiculous!'

Three red triangles flash before his eyes, and suddenly he's got it.

'And besides! My mom didn't lose her tongue! I remember her calling me dove and singing to me. My mom talked!'

'Nami?'

'What?'

'How many boys are there named Nami in Boros? Apart from you?'

'I don't know,' he says softly. 'None, I guess.'

The Old Dame puts a hand on his shoulder.

'Exactly. And this little boy had the same name as you: Nami.'

Nami presses his hands as hard as he can against his eyes and stays that way for several minutes.

'Where is she? That woman? Where is she now?'

***

Nami walks past the bazaar and the job market to go see Majmun. The monkey sits in his cage–in the far corner, generally, where he can't be seen. He listlessly accepts the nuts Nami offers, and retreats back to the corner, where he spends a long time shelling them. His genitals are all red and torn.

On his way back, Nami walks past the port and catches sight of Johnny outside his building. Instead of the wreck on the verge of collapse that Nami is expecting, Johnny looks young and refreshed in a black turtleneck and sunglasses. Treading lightly, like a feral cat, hair blowing in the wind. Nami's breathing quickens. He realises it's not over yet.

# III
# Nymph

Kuce is a village in the middle of the desert, an eleven-hour journey on dirt roads from the capital by bus. A channel for irrigating the cotton fields runs alongside the village. It was dug years ago from the Dere river, which empties into the lake. Wherever Nami looks, he sees nothing but snowy cotton fields: cotton, cotton, cotton. After the long trip, spent sitting next to a woman with a scarf on her head and a sick baby on her lap, he steps off the bus feeling dusty and sore all over.

The village is empty. The co-op market on the village square is closed, as is the beverage stand. Nami walks through the deserted village, peeking in windows, knocking on doors, jiggling door handles. After ten minutes he's made the rounds and walks back to the bus stop. The driver who brought him sits sprawled on the steps of the bus, thick thighs spread wide, smoking a smelly brown cigarette.

'It's cotton harvest, man. Everyone's out in the field,' he drawls in Nami's direction. He spits a streak of brown saliva into the dirt.

'Everyone? You mean like everyone?'

'Well, yeah, you know, nobody gets a pass. You might be ninety, you might have but one leg and one eye, but cotton harvest time comes, you got to get out in the fields and work. Mothers with children, even the mayor. But evening everyone'll be back. Just hold on a while.'

Kuce is a standard village, three dozen squat white homes with corrugated metal roofs arranged in a rectangle around the village square, at the centre of which stands a half-withered mulberry tree. Towering next to it, on a concrete pedestal, is a bronze bust of the Statesman; they couldn't spare the funds for a whole statue in a small village like this. Half a dozen hens wallow in the dirt. At the end of the village is a farm building with a few tin sheds for drying and pressing cotton and a battered truck parked out in front. A flock of sheep. God only knows what they live on. The village has no public lighting, but they do have telephone poles.

The air here is clear, as though it contained nothing at all, just some particles of black desert sand trembling slightly above the ground. Overhead it turns to a dazzling blue. Sounds disappear in the blazing heat like in a vacuum, like when Nami screams into his pillow.

The bus driver empties a bottle of water over his head, grabs a pillow, and shuffles off to take a siesta under the lone tree on the village green. He leaves the bus door open. Who would steal anything here? A few minutes later, Nami hears him snoring away.

Nami walks back down the dirt road from the village to the irrigation canal; even from a distance he can tell it's lined with green thistles. The desert to the left of the canal is all dried up; from here to the horizon a few withered trees are all that's visible. To the right, as far as the eye can see, are fields of fluffy white cotton flowers. The channel from the Dere makes possible two cotton crops a year—a miracle, according to the ubiquitous campaign posters. The water stands motionless in the three-metre-wide concrete irrigation trough. It isn't clean or cold, yet it feels cool to the touch. Tossing aside his travel bag, Nami rolls up his pantlegs and steps into the trough. It's deeper than he expected, his pants end up soaked. But the water evokes joyful feelings, and he catches himself smiling, even if the water is cloudy and kind of stinks. He walks up and down the canal, a hundred metres or so. The bottom is slippery with algae and a thin layer of mud, and every now and then he steps on something sharp.

Nami sits down on the withered grass beside the canal and eats his last three hard-boiled eggs, cooked for him by Vera. He stretches out, inhaling the dust, and closes his eyes against the scorching sun. He wakes a few hours later with a burnt face and a headache. He shields his eyes. The sun now is low. A dusty cloud approaches along the road from the west, turning red. The cotton pickers are returning home. Nami starts to shiver.

***

On one truck ride the men, on another the women and children, and the third and fourth carry sacks of cotton. The people start clambering off the trucks, the youngest and least exhausted folding down the tailgate and leaping to the ground. Somebody tosses them a wooden crate, which they set down in back of the truck, then help the others off. Nobody says much. They're covered in dirt and look worn out. There are children of all ages, including some carried in scarves on the backs of their mothers. Old women, old men. The number of working-age men is surprisingly few.

As he watches the women jumping down off the back of the truck, Nami searches their faces for the familiar features of the one he last saw fourteen years ago. Surveying all the children who might be his half-siblings, he feels a burst of resentment. And then he recognises her. By her singing. Humming to herself as she helps some older women down from the truck. A child crashes into him, Nami staggers, and the woman glances his way. All of a sudden he's no longer sure–the face is completely different from the one he has stored in his mind. Fickle memory! Her blue eyes are what surprises him most. She looks old, much older than she should for her age–and his. He can see she has grey roots, but it's hard to tell if her hair is actually grey or just dusty. The woman looks away and grabs hold of the truck bed.

While the children go running off all over the village, the women head to their homes and the men aim straight for the refreshment stand and order their first shots of liquor. The people here speak quickly, barking almost, as if carrying around some unspoken anger inside of them. It puts Nami a little on edge; he's used to the long, melodious, smooth phrasing of Boros.

The bus driver is sitting up now, leaning his back against the tree, smoking. He'll be heading back to the city soon, but he'll make the trip alone, unless maybe somebody joins him en route in one of the other villages. As the woman walks away, Nami notices something of an old woman's quality to the way she carries herself. Elbows bent close to her body, back hunched, head bowed–this can't be the graceful three triangles. Drawn by her quiet humming, he trails her at a distance of twenty metres. His head is pulsing. He hears the bus starting up behind him.

When the woman reaches her front door–the only one painted green–she turns and looks at him.

'Come on,' she beckons to him. 'I'll make tea.' Nami can see when she speaks that she's missing a few teeth. He holds his breath and follows her into a dark hallway. On one side is a coat rack with a coat and a pair of dress shoes and galoshes underneath on the floor; on the other, a rack of shelves with onions, tomatoes, a bunch of parsley, and some eggplants. Nami takes off his shoes and enters the single-room dwelling. It strikes him as dark and surprisingly cold; simple, like a monastic cell. The floor is earthen, the windows small and high-set. The low bed is spread with a woollen blanket. A short round table and two ottomans are placed next to it. On the opposite wall is an open hearth covered with a cast-iron plate and an opening to the chimney built into the wall above. Hanging on the wall is a small photograph of the lake from the days when it still had plenty of water and trees growing around it, and a kilim-weave rug is draped over a mesh stand underneath.

The woman bends over a small gas cooker, like the one Johnny had for camping, and puts on the water for tea. She leans against the wall and watches the teapot in silence until the water comes to a boil. Then throws in a few leaves of tea, a sprig of some sort of herb, and a heaping spoonful of sugar.

Nami has the feeling the whole thing is unreal. He starts to get dizzy just thinking about where he is and what he's doing. Neither of them says a word. Nami stares intently at her. The woman can only stand it a moment and then averts her gaze.

'Why did you leave me?' he finally says, but it feels like the words were just in his head, that nothing came out of his mouth, so he repeats the question. His voice is clouded, his vocal cords choked with dust.

'Nami,' she says. As if the name itself were a revelation, her eyes widen in surprise. 'Nami,' she repeats. 'Nami.'

Nami presses the hot cup of tea into his palm and squeezes tight.

'Say it again,' he says softly. 'Repeat it.'

And the woman repeats it, saying it over and over, the look on her face almost deranged, calling his name for all the times she didn't have the chance to over the past seventeen years—'Naminaminaminaminaminaminaminami'—until it becomes a mantra, a refrain. Nami sees tears flowing down her cheeks, making little trails through the dust.

'There there,' he says, getting up and wrapping his arms around her. He's half a head taller than her. She smells the same as she did back then, but he already knew she would.

'God, you're so big. You're so big!' she says in disbelief. 'How can you be so big?'

Nami just smiles. He carefully picks her up and lays her on the bed, then kneels down beside her, holding her hand. That's right, he has a mother. A mother all his own, like every other person. The discovery fills him with wonder and disbelief.

'You had a red swimsuit, two-piece,' he says.

'You remember that?'

'I was puking and you held my head.'

His mother smiles.

'There's no beach there anymore. The lake is all shrivelled up.'

She nods. 'That damned cotton is drinking up all the water.'

For a few moments, neither one of them says a word.

'Gramma and Grampa are no longer with us. They're with the Spirit now. The kolkhoz chairman lives in the house. I didn't finish school.'

She stares at him in wonder. 'But you found me though, dove. How in the world did you do it?'

***

It's understood that Nami will stay with the woman. For Nami, she's still *the woman*—or *she,* depending. He's reluctant to call her mother, though he sometimes tries it out in his mind.

The woman runs out of the house and a little while later returns with a leg of lamb with couscous and mint. Nami wolfs it down so fast there are tears in his eyes; he feels like it's the best thing he's ever eaten in his life. The woman watches with a satisfied look as the suet runs down his chin. Then suddenly Nami feels heavy. As if at any moment he's about to fall off the ottoman, and in fact a moment later his body goes limp and he slowly sinks to the floor. The woman puts a cushion under his head and edges the table out of the way to make room for him on the floor. Then she sits for a long time just looking at him, hands folded in her lap.

'How big you are. So strong. And so beautiful,' she whispers softly. The image of his mother's face is foggy and blurred. His head is splitting open, but at least he can finally sleep now. Finally it's over.

He vomits up the entire leg of lamb during the night.

***

The woman departs in the morning before dawn. On the table she leaves him a clay bowl of yogurt with honey. But he's too weak even to raise his arm and spends the whole day lying in bed. The sun beats down through the narrow window into his eyes, but he doesn't have strength to roll out of the way or even cover his face. He sweats so much he feels like his brain is running out his nostrils. It seems ironic that he should die now, when he's finally found his mother, but there's nothing he can do. By the time the woman comes back from the field, he'll be dead meat for sure.

When the woman comes home, the first thing she does is give the place an airing out. For a moment it actually seems like Nami isn't breathing, but then his eyes flutter open.

'Dove,' she says, tears welling up in her eyes.

Nami lies limp, head in the woman's lap, as she spoons mint tea into his mouth, cooling his forehead and quietly singing to him. Then they both fall asleep exhausted. The same pattern repeats over the following days. Nami lies there completely inert, letting the woman take care of him. And she does, without so much as a word, feeding him sweetened tea for hours on end, emptying his chamber pot, changing his sweaty sheets. Mornings she goes out into the fields, but every afternoon she returns with a worried look on her face, walking through the doorway hung with coloured beads in place of a door, to pamper and care for Nami. The weeks go by, the days growing shorter, and the heat waves that once knocked all the energy out of him gradually subside. Nami begins to recover. He sits up in bed and is able to give one-word answers, though his legs are still too weak to carry his weight. Every now and then some of the older women in the village come to look in on him. They bring lamb broth or rice pilaf, and make a comment or two about stiff roots and well-built poplars that go over Nami's head. One day the mayor stops in, a fat, jolly man with a full moustache and a shiny patch on his shirt over his belly, where he constantly rests his folded hands. Nodding his head, he addresses the woman in a lowered voice. Gives a long look at the photo of the lake on the wall, nods again, sighs, and says goodbye.

'What did he say?' asks Nami.

'Nothing,' she replies.

***

One morning the woman wakes him up with a solemn expression on her face. She kneels beside him holding something wrapped in brown paper.

'Happy birthday, dove,' she says in a trembling voice. That's right, Nami's birthday. He can't remember the last time he celebrated. He rubs his eyes and tears open the store-bought wrapping paper. Inside is a bright-yellow stuffed elephant.

The woman shrugs and gives an apologetic smile: 'It was all they had at the co-op.'

'Thank you,' Nami says.

'I'll make you crème caramel when I come home from the field.'

'Thank you, Mom.'

***

By the end of October the cotton is harvested and Nami's mother is staying home longer. She weaves rugs, cultivates the tiny little garden behind her house, and visits the library, which she's in charge of. It's a single dark, musty room, next door to the co-op, open three days a week outside of harvest season. Nami is the only one in the village who ever goes, apart from the broad-faced agronomist who goes to flirt with his mother. Nami reads with the insatiable appetite of a famished beast, picking the books off the shelf in order from left to right; there isn't exactly much there to choose from anyway. National legends, trashy Russian detective fiction, even novels about building socialism, and a handbook on the agronomy of cotton—Nami reads them all.

Nami sits on a hard chair, gobbling up one title after another while his mother walks around the shelves dusting them off with a duster. Every now and then she stops mid-movement, turns and looks at Nami, and slightly shakes her head. Nami watches her out of the corner of his eye. Searching for something he has in common with her. If he looks long and hard enough and really believes, he sees a dimple in her left cheek like his when she smiles. And when she speaks, she has the same singing Boros intonation, though he can sometimes hear the typical Ouroubor bark coming through. He has to settle for that, but it's already much more than he ever dared to dream of. He's living with his own mother–it's actually sort of a miracle.

Once Nami is well again, he starts taking short trips around the area, just nearby the village at first, then gradually increasing his radius. The soil here is parched, the land has been without rain for years. One day he walks out to the tall rocks on the horizon and discovers some trees growing on them with vegetation underneath. He's so surprised and overjoyed he actually starts to laugh.

Might it actually be possible for things to happen in harmony with Nami instead of going against him? For him to have a quiet, boring, ordinary life? For the Spirit of the Lake to finally get tired and stop paying attention to him? For him to finally live with somebody who loves him and occasionally be able to decide things for himself? Just the little things would be enough–say, whether he would go for a walk or play soccer with the boys in the village, or lie down in bed and stare up at the ceiling until it made his eyes hurt. Or to see mist again someday. Just a few little bits of happiness would totally be enough.

Nami lies down in the moss and discovers the tiny fruit of some late-season cowberries, which he picks and puts into his pocket to bring back to his mother. By the time he gets home, it's dark.

'Here,' says Nami, emptying the contents of his pocket into his mother's hand. The berries are frozen like little ice beads.

'The mayor said when sowing begins, you'll have to go out in the fields along with everybody else,' Nami's mother says casually. Nami just kicks off his shoes and pours himself a cup of tea.

'Assuming you're fully recovered, of course,' his mother

adds. Nami lowers his head and squints up at her: 'They told me you lost your tongue.'

'It's true,' his mother says, wiping her face with a corner of her scarf. The desert dust is constantly getting stuck in her wrinkles, like it does to everyone here. 'Let me make you some rice–'

'Tell me what happened,' Nami interrupts.

His mother shakes her head. 'Rice pilaf.'

She cooks rice pilaf with lamb offal and cowberries.

***

The days are turning shorter and distinctively cool. Nami puts on his footwraps and sets out to the desert each morning. The cotton fields are harvested, the plants ploughed under, the soil turned and quiet. There is a special brightness to the winter air, and its acoustic properties are extraordinary; sounds travel a long way and seem harsher, as if they were propagating through metal particles. A stray dog accompanies Nami on his travels now; to judge from his paws and his playfulness he seems to be still young. Nami silently puts up with him. Every so often he throws him a stick. Then one day he starts to give him commands and the dog obeys. He knows exactly what Nami wants. So one day Nami brings the dog home and over his mother's protests lets him sleep in the hallway. It's their first clash of wills, and Nami refuses to back down. Eventually his mother gives in, in spite of her fear of the dog. The dog snores loudly at night.

One night Nami is woken by shouting and loud voices. He jumps out of bed, tripping over the dog, and runs out the door. The village square is filled with Ouroubors holding flashlights and lanterns, their wide faces and large, flat noses turned to the sky. Yes, it really is–rain. Children scamper through the crowd in their nightshirts, screaming wildly. It's a soft rain, not even enough to make puddles, but that does nothing to dampen the villagers' joy. They take off their clothes, exposing themselves to the cold rain as if it were manna from heaven. Nami stands, head tipped back, pointing a flashlight upward as he watches the raindrops falling down through the cone of light. The mayor passes through the crowd, nudging and winking at them as if it were his doing. A thin old lady bursts into a fit of mad laughter that turns first to sobs, then to uncontrolled weeping. Nami sees two women dancing.

'I can't remember the last time I saw rain,' Nami tells his mother. 'I can't remember the last time I saw people this happy.'

'Allah!' the agronomist cries. 'Allah is merciful!'

His mother keeps quiet.

***

The next day his mother accompanies him on his walk into the desert. There's no sign of the rain whatsoever. The desert is as dry as ever, only the air is a little damper. The dog merrily runs ahead, stopping every few dozen metres and pricking up his ears, urging them to pick up the pace. As usual, neither of them says a word. The ecstatic experience of the night before rests between them like an invisible boulder.

The dog sniffs the air, pauses bewildered, bounds forward twice, and spots his prey: a tiny desert cat. But it's much faster than him and knows the terrain far better.

'We could go back to Boros,' Nami suggests.

His mother trembles, drawing her woollen scarf more closely about her body.

'This place is hell. A dried-up piece of ground where even

a thistle doesn't grow. People shouldn't be here in the first place. What are we doing slaving away for the Russians here when they're the ones who drove all these people out of their homes? It doesn't make any sense!'

His mother stops and turns to him. Her nostrils are quivering. 'What does make sense, Nami? Tell me. What does make sense in life?'

The dog yaps furiously. Nami can feel his fingers going numb. 'Quiet, stupid!' he shouts at the dog. Not a cloud in the sky, once again. Nami euphorically recalls the night before, wondering if he just dreamed the cold rain falling on his face. He remembers those rare days back at school when it snowed and the teacher let them go outside; they stood in the schoolyard, heedlessly dressed, catching snowflakes on their tongue, or, if there was more snow they lay down in it and made faceprints, or sculpted the snow into obscene figures, until their sleeves were soaking wet and the teacher shooed them back into the classroom to dry off by the stove. It seems like so long ago now.

'I can't go back to Boros, dove.'

'Why not? Why?!'

The dog turns around with a frightened look and tucks his tail between his legs.

'My God, Nami. Be quiet already. Stop screaming. I will never go back to the lake.'

Then again neither one of them says a word as they walk on through the dust. They both look ahead, avoiding each other's eyes.

***

She was so young! How old could she have been? Seventeen? Yes, of course, seventeen. Not even legally an adult. She had never tried vodka, not even tobacco! Classes at school were still mixed in those days, boys and girls together. Of course it led to nothing good, there were all sorts of trouble.

Of course there had been teasing between them. She herself had once hit a boy who wouldn't leave her alone and kept lifting up her skirt. She smacked him so hard she split open his eyebrow and had to report to the principal's office, but she wasn't about to put up with that sort of thing. Then there was this one boy who really shouldn't even have been in a normal school. He was handicapped, and by handicapped, she meant seriously, not just a little. He would sing to himself in falsetto, waving his hands around, or sometimes he liked to arrange things on his desk—chestnuts, stones, pencils—in some special order that only he understood, and if anyone messed them up he would go totally insane and start banging his head on the bench till he bled. A boy like that shouldn't even go to school, at least not with normal children. Was she right or was she right? It was only natural that the other kids harassed him, lighting his notebooks on fire and pissing on his homework, that's just how it is when somebody's weird.

Nami suddenly realises he's walking next to a girl who's probably about the same age as he is, chatting away like she was with her clique of friends. Her movements and gestures were no longer those of an old person. Even her facial expressions had become much more lively.

And so this one young man took a fancy to his mother. She wasn't sure how it happened, she definitely didn't do anything to provoke his interest, but the boy started following her home every day. He would wait for her in front of the school, then pull her close and give her a hug. He gave her clear candies and sea glass from the lake. Her classmates made fun of her when they saw. It was annoying, but actually he was so dumb that she wasn't even that mad about it. It wouldn't have done any good, anyway, since he was too stupid to comprehend when she tried to tell him. She tried chasing him away, she tried pinching him and telling him to go home, she tried laughing at him and mocking him—he didn't understand. It was impossible.

Nami can feel the tension growing inside him, noticing his posture getting more and more upright. He's shivering so much with cold the muscles in his chest hurt.

His mother is suddenly colder too, pausing her story to rub her fingers.

'Let's go back,' she suggests, and Nami nods silently. Even just nodding he realises his neck is stiff.

'He isn't my father, is he?'

His mother pauses. 'There was nothing I could do, dove. It isn't my fault. He hid between the buildings and waited for me on my way home. It was January, almost dark out. He jumped me from behind ...'

Nami sniffles. The sun is starting to go down. The first lights are coming on in the village in the distance. They walk in silence. His mother takes him by the arm and suddenly she's that old woman again, even though on paper she's only thirty-five.

'What's his name? Do I know him?' Nami asks after a few moments.

'Shahnaz. His name was Shahnaz.'

'Is he dead?'

'He's with the Spirit of the Lake.'

'What happened to him?'

His mother sighs. 'What happened? I wove fifteen, maybe twenty rugs before I was able to speak again. I'm not able to talk about it.'

'Come on, let's pick up the pace,' Nami says. 'Where's that dog?'

'Wait. Just wait.'

She stands out of breath, trying to grab a strand of hair that's slipped out from under her scarf.

'They came for him that same evening and pulled him out of bed. His mom screamed and yelled and threw herself at the men who came to take her son, but what could she do against them? They beat him and lynched him, then tossed him into the lake.'

'The lake,' Nami breathes. He stops to give her a hug. They stand there paralysed, Nami feeling the cold spreading through his body. After all the effort he put into finding his mother, he has to support her now. The uneasiness is back, nothing has been resolved, he can't stop yet.

'Do you blame yourself?' he asks after a while.

'I had no idea what they'd do to him. I never would've told anyone if I'd known what they would do.'

'It isn't your fault. Barbarians. Them and their fucking people's courts.'

He pauses a moment. 'So then what?' Nami asks, though he's already heard all he wants to know.

His mother shrugs, 'Nothing. My parents put me on a bus to the capital that very night. They knew once those men sobered up, they would try to pin the blame on me. And they did. The bad harvest, the water drying up in the lake, a bad day at sea—it was all a result of that crime, which I had been the cause of. The Lake Spirit was angry and had to be fed. His mouth needed filling.'

'Savages,' Nami says. 'They would've sacrificed you too.'

His mother shrugs. 'Probably. We weren't about to wait to find out.'

The lights of the village flicker in the distance, but everything seems slowed down, the night liquid and heavy. With the climate changing less often in the desert, Nami was more perceptive to every tiny shift. Sometimes he found himself sniffing the air like that stupid dog. He even tried to prick up his ears. Now, though, Nami is cold and shaking with rage. His mother hangs on his arm, as if yielding control of her body to him. She tells him how she met her husband among the Ouroubors. He was crude and uncouth, but he loved her. When they moved to the desert, he started drinking and beating her. He knocked out a few of her teeth and caused her to miscarry the child she was expecting with him. Finally, one night on his way home from the local dive, he fell into the irrigation canal and drowned. She had had peace ever since, and no, she didn't want to change it. So that was it, that was her whole life. She would never go back to the lake. Now she's cold and tired and just wants to get home as soon as possible.

***

Exhausted as he is, that night Nami can't get to sleep. He decides to get up and go for a walk and finds his mother sitting on the bed, back against the wall, hands folded in her lap. He sits down beside her and stays that way till daybreak. Toward morning, they fall asleep on each other's shoulders, wedged together like two ripe poppy heads, breathing in the same rhythm and dreaming the same, wild dreams.

***

The villagers have been restless ever since the night it rained. They gather in the square often now, holding long, impassioned discussions, even in the dark, and the mayor has to send dispatches about it to headquarters, which makes him sweat just that much more and his smile is even more visibly fake. Sowing begins in a month, and the last thing he needs is to have to deal with any disturbances. Over the course of a week, their debates result in a list of three demands: Fridays off from work for prayer, build a mosque on the square, and they want to bury their deceased in the graveyard with their foreheads toward Mecca. The mayor asks wryly whether now that they're so pious, they won't be drinking vodka in the dive anymore, but the frowning faces that greet his remark convince him to abandon any further attempts at humour. He diligently writes to headquarters. It rains lightly again. There are disputes over whether this is a good sign or a bad sign.

When sowing time comes, the men refuse to get on the truck and go out to the fields until the mayor agrees to their demands. The mayor, who has up to now kept hidden from them the fact that headquarters denied their requests, loses his temper and yells at them that they should be glad they have something to eat. The men look around at each other a moment, then grumblingly climb in the back of the truck. They do a sloppy job of planting, though, flinging most of the seeds to the wind. Then they sit down in the furrows and yak, just casually shooting the breeze. Nami sits not far away, munching on a snack. The agronomist moans and groans while the mayor clenches his fists.

After a while, the men stand up, go back to the truck, and tear the propaganda banner off the tailgate about raising cotton yields. Two young men Nami's age start jumping up and down on the sign and dance the kazachok.

'Guys, are you crazy?' the mayor says, throwing up his hands. 'You're gonna get us in trouble! We're all friends here, aren't we? You wanna make me call headquarters and have them send in the army? Come on, don't be stupid. Just get back to work and we can forget all about it.'

The men pay him no attention, just standing around smoking. Then they hop up on the back of the truck and one of them pounds the cab. 'Headin home!'

The driver climbs in and starts the engine. All the rest of the men, including the mayor, climb on board. It's seven kilometres to the village, after all. No one wants to walk.

***

There are reports of Ouroubors rebelling in other villages too. No word from headquarters, just dead silence. The cotton fields lie fallow and by early spring there are weeds popping up left and right. The men start construction work on the mosque, evenings sitting around the village square, drinking vodka and wondering where to dig up a cleric. They decide they want the women to cover their hair now, but some say even that's not enough, they should also cover their faces.

'Take a hike,' Nami's mother says through her teeth, though she already wears a scarf over her hair anyway. When the men get drunk, they yell things at her, like they do at all the other women in the village. They start growing in beards and acting important.

The supply truck that normally delivers groceries to the village now runs only sporadically. The mail service and the buses are no longer working at all. One morning, the bust of the Statesman is doused in red paint. The mayor has his things packed and ready to go, but headquarters won't allow him to leave his post, saying they need him to file reports on the progressive decline in morality. One morning he arrives at his office to find a cross painted and crossed-out on his door in motor oil and a frog nailed to the door. Through waiting, the mayor takes one of the trucks and simply drives away.

The co-op market is totally empty at this point, and the kiosk that sells alcohol has been drunk dry. The only thing in the village still functioning is the library, which nobody goes to. The bust of the Statesman lies in the dust; sprouting up around it are a few sickly stalks of wormwood, to spite the desert. Nami's mother hoes the soil in her garden, planting beans, potatoes, carrots, and onions, making sure they'll have something to eat. She trades one of her kilims for three hens and another for two bags of nuts and a half-dozen jars of honey.

'We have to get away,' Nami says to his mother every day, but she just tosses her head. She has everything she needs here. The men will calm down soon enough, and everything will go back to the way it was before.

The mosque still isn't finished. Construction on the minaret collapsed when they ran out of material and now it appears to be bowing a little to one side. The men never neglect to point out that it's tipping toward Mecca. Spring is in the air. Hardy spurge sprouts among the rows of the ploughed fields, and a desert lark can be seen capering about.

There are days when Nami goes hours without remembering love, but with the coming of spring his desire intensifies. He hears a moan in the creaking of a door, the fold of a towel can call to mind a woman's sex. He recognises his torment in the silly folk songs the Ouroubor women sing while waiting their turn to draw water at the spring. He has vivid dreams. Dreams of Zaza, of entering her, rising up on his arms so he can see them joining together. Then he sinks back onto her, so he can hold her close and love her with all his being is capable of. There is never a climax in his dreams, so most of the time he wakes with an erection, then pounds the pillow in rage. He covers his mouth with his own arm and moans into it. Sometimes he bites down until he draws blood.

***

'We have to get away,' he tells his mother.

She objects, saying she doesn't want to start over again, she has everything she needs here, and the men have settled down. They've even begun to talk about sowing the cotton fields after all. The harvest would be late, but at least it would be something, they still needed to live.

'I have to go back to Boros,' Nami says finally, giving his mother a pleading look. She doesn't say a word. That night she cries, but she knows she can never go back to the lake. She doesn't say goodbye to him when he leaves, plunging back into speechlessness.

# IV

# Imago

The journey to the capital is long and tiring. It takes him nearly a week; he covers long stretches on foot, then hitch-hikes some of the way. One day Nami sees a burned village in the distance. A few times he's passed by Russian military convoys. The soldiers are closemouthed, lost in their own thoughts. The desert seems to be endless, creeping up to the very edge of the capital itself. The city greets him with an eerie silence, charred car wrecks lining the roads, shop windows broken or boarded up. The stalls at the bazaar have been abandoned and overturned, strips of newspaper, torn apart and twisted into cones for the sale of roasted sunflower seeds, float through the air

The garden wall at the Old Dame's house is half-demolished, the trees he once pruned broken, the flower beds trampled. Nami arrives to find the Old Dame sitting on the veranda drinking tea from a porcelain mug. Vera sits at her feet like a loyal dog. The Old Dame gets up and gives him a hug, pressing her hot palms against his cheeks. She says how much she worried about him, how glad she is to have him back, that terrible things had happened.

'Those Ouroubor riffraff destroyed the garden. They trampled and pillaged everything before the police could come–God, I never dreamed I would call the bloody police. Do you know what they did?' she says indignantly to Nami. 'They tore down the drawing room curtains and shat on top of them. They smashed the sugar bowl from Paris against the wall. They took the ginger biscuits I eat for flatulence and dumped them out on the floor and crushed them under their boots. Can you comprehend it?'

Vera, red-eyed, sobs that the Ouroubors are savages and pigs, that they attacked the city that fed them and supported them. Good thing the army cracked down on them, they did so much damage ...

'They can't even do a revolution properly!' the Old Dame shouted, then sent Vera off to warm up some milk and honey for Nami. She says the Ouroubors are uneducated animals, to be pitied rather than hated.

'I don't actually like milk with honey,' Nami says in an apologetic tone.

'Oh really? Why didn't you say so before?'

He shrugs.

Then the Old Dame tells Nami how she was sitting at the piano in the drawing room of her pillaged home, playing Chopin's Nocturne in E-flat major, when a three-man patrol from the Russian army burst in.

'Two of them were boys not much older than you. Their uniforms were covered in dust. You could tell they felt awkward, swinging their big paws around like bears in the circus. Even with everything all smashed up, it was obvious this was the fanciest place they'd ever been. These were boys from some churchless village where they bathe in rain-water once a month,' the Old Dame says in disgust.

'They had a lieutenant, a thin man of about forty, with this gloomy face and tremendous eyebrows. I completely ignored them until after I was done playing the last note. Then I looked up and saw him there, frowning like a factory man on a working Saturday. At any rate, finally it came out that they had come here looking for water.'

The Old Dame staidly adjusts the cameo brooch on her chest. 'So the two boys went into the kitchen for water, and the lieutenant points to the piano and asks if he can give it a try. Now you know I didn't want that ruffian anywhere near my keyboard. My daddy had that piano brought here all the way from Berlin!'

Nami watches Vera sitting on the stone step of the veranda, poking her finger into a run in her stockings. A big bird sits heavily on a fig tree branch.

'"May I?" asked the lieutenant. So polite and well-behaved. So I let him sit down. At which point he bowed like he was in some concert hall somewhere and proceeded to play, if you can imagine, another nocturne by Chopin, the Nocturne in H major. He had such long, noble fingers, just like Rachmaninoff!'

'He played beautifully,' Vera sighs. The Old Dame gives her a disgruntled look.

'Of course he played beautifully. I could tell very well his playing was much better than mine. Vera's jaw was on the floor, and so was the soldiers'—they stood in the doorway gaping. And you know what he said to me when he was done?' The Old Dame leans forward toward Nami. '"Pardon me," he said. He said he used to be a professor at the conservatory and he was apologising because he hadn't practiced in so long. He looked as if he was about to burst into tears any moment. So then one of the soldiers blurted out that the water wasn't running—the poor man, trying to cover up for the embarrassment of his commanding officer! It really was quite touching.'

The Old Dame pauses. In the distance, a siren wails, high to low and back again. Nami looks down at his hands, but his vision is out of focus.

'I asked him if it was Ouroubor blood he had on his uniform,' she goes on. 'There was this dark stain on his chest, you see? He just smiled wearily and told me, Good lord, no, it was just motor oil. But he said everyone had their blood on their hands.'

'I heard there's a pit outside the city where all those barbaric poor devils are buried,' Vera blurts out. Her voice jumps over and Nami winces.

'I told him what I thought of them,' the Old Dame continues, shaking her head disapprovingly. 'I told him they were scum. *Svolotch takaya*! I said, so that he would understand. So he wouldn't think he could fix it by playing the piano. But I also told him to keep playing. Vera brought in the cognac, we drank a toast. Then the lieutenant sat back down on the stool, raised his fingers over the keyboard, and started playing 'Ochi chyornye'! My God, how he played! His hands were running up and down those keys from right to left like they were oiled by the devil! Then he downed a glass of cognac and proceeded to play 'Dve gitary' and a few other Gypsy songs, head back, eyes closed. He just drank and played till he fell off the stool.' The Old Dame nodded. 'And those two little soldiers just sat there on that brocade upholstery quietly. One of them fell asleep and started snoring under his breath, but the other one was listening with his mouth open. On their way out they had to prop up their lieutenant to keep him from falling. Nami, are you listening to me?'

Nami is asleep.

***

'I'll help you get your place back into its original state,' Nami says later.

'You're a kind boy.'

'I'm happy to do it.'

Vera brings sweet mint tea and Nami tells the Old Dame how he finally found his mother, and yes, how happy he is about it, although it is a little strange, and yes, they love each other and it's really nice being together, yes, in a way they're very close, but there's something between them that's been broken for good. The Old Dame gives a slight cough, nodding as if this was what she'd expected all along.

'I suppose you have another trip ahead of you now?'

Nami nods. Yes, he has to go to Boros. He has, ahem, relatives there ...

'It'll wait,' the Old Dame says. 'Just relax for now.'

Nami collapses into a heap of dusty comforters, wishing with all his heart that he'll wake up to find the last few fucking years have all just been a dream.

***

A state of emergency has been declared. The only cars driving through the streets are the police. They stop Nami and check his papers several times. The homeless people and stray dogs have all disappeared. The shops are looted and closed. Where the job market used to be is now deserted. The park is full of garbage, some of the benches have been flipped over. The walls, even the stone bear statue in the city park, have been spray-painted with slogans for Ouroubor independence, most of them with spelling mistakes and barely legible. Some of them have already been painted over in green. When Nami reaches the baboon cage, he finds the bars pried open and the cage inside empty. Then he takes a step closer and sees him: a ball of fur huddled right up next to the ceiling on a branch with a tyre hanging down on a chain.

Nami cries out for joy. 'Majmun!' He can't remember the last time he was so happy to see someone. 'Majmun, you old son of a bitch, c'mere! Your cage is open, man. Come on out. Come with me, I'll take care of you. Let's go!'

Majmun stirs, then turns and watches Nami intently.

'Do you recognise me, Majmun? You know who I am,

don't you? I used to bring you fruits and nuts, remember?'

The baboon gazes at him indifferently, then turns his head away.

'Hey, look what I have here! A peanut! Hello! Majmun!'

Slowly and cautiously, the monkey moves toward him. He takes the nut from Nami, then quickly retreats with it to his corner, where he sits crunching away, no longer paying Nami any attention.

'Majmun! Can't you see?! You're free!'

Majmun starts tugging at his penis and screeching angrily.

***

Nami sits out on the concrete pier, watching the dockers lounging around the sidings that lead from the freight train station to port. Clumps of yellowy grass sprout up between the ties now that no more freight is running along the rails. It's been ages since the men had anything to do, but they're used to coming here, so they come and smoke together in silence. Every so often one of the workers shouts something out and a shrill crescendo of voices meets him in response, but Nami can't understand what they say.

He sits on the edge of the pier, munching roasted chick-peas. To his right is a concrete path leading down to the lake; it used to be a dry dock. At the point where the ramp starts to incline, an off-road vehicle is parked, shiny and clean. He doesn't doubt it for a second; it's Johnny's car. Same silver grille and dual headlights. Johnny must have come to the port to see his dealer. He would be walking back this way in a moment, his pockets full of coke and heroin. How could Nami have thought he would never see him again?

The car gleams in the sun like the armour of the Golden Horde. Johnny's darling, the personification of his hunger and his success. He felt more for that hunk of metal than he ever had for any person in his life. He'd never even showed that much affection for his stupid cat.

Obviously Nami knew where Johnny kept his spare key stashed. Obviously he could get in the car, take it out of park, and give it a little shove. Given the angle of the ramp, the car would gain enough speed to break through the surface. Enough for the foul-smelling lake water to get in the open door and ruin the leather seats and expensive stereo. For the engine to get so clogged with mud it would never start again. Nami takes a quick glance around and assesses the situation. About fifty metres to the car from him, he can make it. He takes off at a sprint. A tanker blows its horn in the distance, giving Nami a start. He feels around the left front wheel and finds the key almost immediately. Wrapped in plastic and stuck to the body with several layers of tape. His index finger brushes against something sharp and he hisses in pain. He pulls it out and sees that it's bleeding. Swears quietly. He lies down under the front bumper and tries to wrest the key out with his other hand. It's stuck down with at least five strips of gaffer's tape. Nami peels them off one by one, working blind, first inserting a nail between the tape and the metal, then taking the tape between his thumb and finger and ripping it free.

When he gets back to his feet, his hands are scratched and filthy, but clutched in his fist is a plastic bag with a thick layer of dirt on it. He steps up to the driver's side of the car and looks at his reflection in the dark, smoky glass. What the fuck am I doing? he thinks. He closes his eyes and drops the hand with the spare key to his side. Then takes a deep breath, cocks his arm, and hurls the keys into the lake with all his might. The surface is too far away for him to reach, of course, but the key lands in the mud with a smack and quickly gets sucked under.

It's like shedding fifty kilos: Nami takes a deep breath and straightens up his back. He sees Johnny come walking out of a warehouse building with a slow, leisurely, springy step, almost like he was bouncing. If the Spirit of the Lake actually existed, Nami thinks to himself, Johnny would have to have a huge tumour on his neck, or at the very least have his hair fall out or eczema on his face. From a distance, though, Johnny looks as young, fresh, and healthy as ever.

'Hi, Johnny,' Nami says, maybe a bit too loudly.

Johnny looks up in surprise. His eyes are hidden behind the lenses of his sunglasses.

'Nami. You scoundrel.'

They size each other up with their eyes, neither of them saying a word. The wind picks up, bringing with it a cloud of toxic dust. Nami covers his face with his elbow. 'I can't see your eyes,' he says.

Johnny takes off his glasses slowly and nonchalantly. His hand is slightly shaking. He holds his glasses by the frame just in front of his chest, making no attempt to hide his annoyance at their meeting.

Nami drops his hand to his side as if preparing to draw a revolver.

They stare into each other's eyes, long and hard. Johnny's pupils are dilated. It's starting to get hot and both of them are sweating. Nami can feel his heartbeat in every part of his body.

Johnny looks away. 'Fuck you!' he says. 'This isn't the Wild West, you twerp.'

Nami smiles and walks away. After a few steps, he hears Johnny start whistling to himself. It sounds hopelessly forced. As Johnny drives off in his shiny car, the dock workers watch in silence, spitting into the dust at their feet.

***

Over the next few weeks, Nami repairs the damage to the Old Dame's garden. He cuts down the ruined trees, planting new ones in their place ('Will I ever eat cherries from them again?' the Old Dame asks, half in jest and half in sadness). He retills and weeds the flower beds. He fills in a missing chunk of garden wall, not artfully perhaps but solidly, and plants a climbing bougainvillea next to it. But water is increasingly difficult to access, so many of his plants dry up before the Old Dame can enjoy them.

He tells her that the rose next to the gazebo bloomed overnight.

'And what are the blossoms like, tell me!' the Old Dame inquires excitedly. Nami just nods, so she quickly changes into her shoes and practically runs outside to see them for herself. The stem of the rose is thin and weak as if it had been ill but dripping with lush green leaves and crimson petals.

'One of them is white, isn't it?' says the Old Dame, her voice shaking for the first time since Nami has known her. He nods. The Old Dame bends over and gingerly touches the one white bud on the stem of the special rose. She explains that every year they would wait for this moment when her daddy would come to the garden and shout, 'The white rose is blooming!' and everyone would come running out, and then they drank tea in the gazebo with lavender biscuits, and everyone would delight in the anomaly of a white blossom, as white as her dress and the dresses of her sisters, blooming on the stem of a red rose. Her daddy would smile from behind his glasses and her mum would clap and pour out the tea into the porcelain cups from Paris. When had she last seen the rose bloom? She couldn't even remember ...

Her chin quivers a moment as she loses herself in reverie.

'My dear Nami, you have given me back my joy. I feel like I'm alive again! Here I had thought ... when those savages destroyed it all, I felt like everything was covered in slime. That I would never be able to touch it again. That I could no longer live here. But I can. Bit by bit, one gets back on one's feet, doesn't one?' The Old Dame laughs and lights a cigarette in a holder. 'And that rose now? My God, I could never have hoped for such a thing!'

'It's possible they may lift the state of emergency within a week and you could go to Boros,' she says after a moment.

Nami would like to invite her to come with him. But he knows he can't ask that of her. He has to go alone. It is a trip he greatly fears.

***

The buses aren't running, Nami has to go on foot.

The road is a dusty one, trimmed here and there with a sickly yellow star-of-Bethlehem or blue speedwell. Every so often he runs across the rusted wreck of a car, vegetation pushing up through its chassis. What happened to the passengers? Nami wonders. Did they run out of gas or get a flat tyre and there was nobody there to help? Were they held up by bandits? Or by a Russian with a rifle who'd run out of cigarettes? And now were they all being eaten by wild animals? Peeking into one of the cars, Nami sees a purple plastic sandal and a cheap pair of sunglasses with broken frames.

Every now and then the road climbs up a hillside. Nami discovers the charred skeleton of a bus, lying on its side, on the slope of one such hill.

He remembers when he was little his grampa sometimes used to take him on short trips outside of town and they never had to worry about water; there was always a fountain along every road, fed by a spring. Usually there was also a tin can attached to it on a chain. Yes, those were things they took for granted. Now all the fountains were dried up and useless, and basins at their feet empty, apart from mounds of wind-blown dust.

There is dust everywhere, raining down from all sides. It clings to tree branches, blades of grass, beetles' wing covers, Nami's mucous membranes, even the backs of his hands. It pours into his boots through his shoelace holes.

Fishing villages sit in the distance on the hillsides, hundreds of metres away now from the lake's oily surface. Deep cracks run through the earth from the villages down to the water, like the scars left behind by acute abdominal surgery. When the wind blows off the lake, there is an ugly stench to it.

Nami walks and walks till he has blisters on his feet. They gradually fill with water and blood, then burst and soak into the leather of his boots. By the third day he's used to it. Spring is in full swing. In the daytime the temperature breaks thirty degrees, but at night it tends to be chilly. Nami at this point is numb to feelings of heat, cold, pain, hunger, they reach him only in muffled whispers, as if through a thick potato sack. He seeks out sleeping places like an animal, to ensure he'll be protected from as many sides as possible, crawling into low undergrowth or under a rocky overhang. As long as they last, he eats the salted cheese, nuts, and dried apricots he got from the Old Dame. When he runs across a brook flowing out of the woods, he remembers how the boys used to hunt trout in the stream under Kolos Mountain; he makes his hands into a V and carefully runs them through the space beneath the rocks along the bank. Good fortune smiles on him and he actually lands on a fish, though it's so undersized he can barely keep a grip on it. He tosses it onto the bank, and the little trout almost thrashes itself back into the water before Nami grabs hold of his pocketknife and, panting and out of breath, runs it through behind the gills.

At the foot of a tree, Nami finds a squirrel's nest, and sets some dry leaves on fire underneath. As the squirrels come running out, disconcerted and blinded, Nami is waiting, stick in hand, ready to strike.

That evening as he roasts his dinner over a tiny flame—wood is desperately scarce and he barely finds enough to cook the meat halfway—he sees another, much more massive fire over the lake. Spectacular balls of fire explode into an enormous wall of flame as Nami wearily bites into the tough chunks of flesh, taking in the show. From the tall towers he can tell it's a refinery, and judging from the layout probably the one outside the capital. But that's impossible. How could he be seeing something happening in the capital when he's already a week's travel away?

As he stares out over the water, it suddenly hits him: a mirage. Thanks to the reflection he can see what's happening more than a hundred and fifty kilometres away: ruination and destruction—the Apocalypse, as his grampa would say. The capital is burning.

He hears the crackle of his own modest little fire as he sees the flames over half the sky. He can smell his own sweat. He chews the meat of a squirrel's thigh.

***

He thinks he can see Boros in the distance. Beyond it the crag of Kolos, though it seems smaller than he remembers. Fishermen's Lane, the Russian housing estate, smaller; the roads narrower. He rubs his eyes a moment, it's like he's reached some other town. A tiny town, for children. But the interplanetary transmitter is still standing there on the hill where it used to be. There can be no doubt: Nami has made it to Boros.

The closer he gets to town the faster Nami walks, but the

proportions remain unchanged. The buildings shrunk while he was away, the distances are shorter. Only the lake has receded so far that the water is barely visible. Nami keeps his eyes on it, convinced the lake has just drawn back the way the sea retreats before a tsunami hits, and that any minute now it's going to wash them all away. But, glistening in the distance, the surface remains motionless. Stretching almost all the way off to the horizon is a fleet of rusting cargo ships, sunken into the crust of dried mud, camels resting in their shade.

The fish processing plant is closed, its rusty gate, draped in a motivational banner, on the point of collapse. Self-sown trees grow in the yard.

The school classroom is empty, the desks still there, but the chairs are gone, blackboard hanging by its corner from a single nail. The windows are all broken and fallen off their hinges. The door will never close again.

The prefab tenement houses left behind by the Russians are full of wind-blown dust. None of them have windows, though there still appear to be people living in some of the apartments. You can see clear through to the other side. Inside, the apartments are bare, not a tile on the wall. The roulette wheel in the once so popular casino is so covered in dust it no longer spins.

Nami goes to hang around in front of Zaza's building, a two-storey apartment house with a peeling facade. He sits down on the curb the way he used to, hawking phlegm into the dust and waiting for a Russian army jeep to drive by, so he can spray it with a round from his machine gun. The only thing that comes down the road all afternoon, though, is one old granny with a scabby goat and some kids carrying groceries. Nami realises his hands are itchy and starts scratching himself again.

***

Zaza comes home toward evening. Carrying a basket of eggs and with no bow on her head, but a dark blue scarf. A shiny purse is slung over her shoulder, an unquestionable sign of adulthood. As the sunlight falls on her from behind, Nami can see her silhouette, still slim and girlish, underneath her dress, though she's lost some spring in her step.

'Zaza,' he says.

She glances at him in surprise, but the moment she sees that it's him, smiles. She stretches out her hand as if about to stroke his cheek, but then just tucks a strand of hair back into her scarf. The eggs jiggle inside the basket. Each one is individually wrapped in newsprint.

'Nami. When did you get here?'

'Yesterday. Well, actually today.'

Zaza smiles, he guesses probably at his nervousness.

'How are you, Zaza? I often ... you know ...' his voice cracks.

'I'm fine, Nami. Thank you.'

'That's good.'

'I am in a hurry, though.'

Nami wonders where she could be going in such a hurry. Everything happens in slow motion in Boros, like a fly stuck in honey. 'Sure. See you tomorrow?'

Zaza gives a quick glance at the door of her building, then up at the window.

'I don't know.'

'Whatever you say.'

Zaza stands with the basket of eggs braced against her right hip.

'I gotta go.'

'Wait a sec.'

'What?'

'I don't know. Don't go yet.'

'I have to.'

Nami notices that her hands are shaking. The way they used to when he touched her on the back of her neck or her shoulders. That's a long time ago now. 'I see you've still got that eczema ... On your hands.'

'Yeah. The drier the lake is, the worse it gets.'

'Hm. More and more toxins in it every day, right?'

Zaza gives him a blank look and scratches at her wrist.

'Come to the candy store tomorrow, yeah?'

Zaza shrugs. She shoves open the door with her shoulder in a funny way that reminds Nami of a goatling pushing into a pen. Arm awkwardly gripping the basket of eggs from above. She's still a child, Nami realises. Anyway, I was blabbering on in front of her like a schoolboy.

He has to smile at that.

***

He runs into the usual familiar faces that gaze at him indifferently, just like Majmun the monkey–he's not in their sphere of interest. Says hello to his former schoolteacher who stares at him in shock. She's carrying a large package with a ribbon, probably a gift. She takes a few steps past him, then turns around and says, 'Nami?!' He smiles back at her, but after a while they realise they have nothing to say to each other, and they go along their separate ways.

Nami feels his breath quicken when he sees the house where he grew up. The railing on the stoop is painted in a bright blue that hurts his eyes to look at. A flowerpot sits in the way of the entrance. The moment Nami sees it, he decides he's going to pee on the flowers till they wither and die. There are comforters airing out in the upstairs window, and baby clothes hanging on the clothesline. The front door is wide open. He can hear music on the radio coming from inside.

Nami shifts his knapsack onto his other shoulder and knocks on the door. He waits a moment but nobody answers, so he goes ahead inside. The room is freshly painted, and the child with three hands sits beneath the table, playing with something that Nami can't see. The child looks up, and seeing Nami, laughs out loud. A cradle stands along the wall; the kolkhoz chairman must have had another child. His wife stands at the stove, sideways to Nami, smiling to herself. She actually looks decent in profile. Nami clears his throat and the woman gives a start.

'Hello,' Nami says.

'Good day,' the woman replies, her smile giving way to a look of concern. 'Have a seat. The soup will be ready soon.'

'Did you have another baby?'

The woman nods, wiping the sweat on her forehead.

'Congratulations.'

The woman just frowns at him.

'Another little boy?'

'A girl.'

'Well, that's good, isn't it? A matching set, right?' Nami searches his memory for all the phrases he remembers his gramma used to say.

'Yes.'

The woman regards Nami impassively as he approaches the cradle. Asleep inside is a little girl with a full head of curly hair, an angelic expression on her face, and just one arm. Where the other arm should be is a palm with four fingers jutting out of the shoulder. Nami closes his eyes for a moment and holds his breath.

'The Spirit of the Lake is still angry,' the woman says quietly.

'God forbid he not be,' Nami mutters to himself. He sits down and folds his hands on top of the table.

'The soup is kohlrabi,' the woman says. Nami nods. The child under the table tugs at the bottom of Nami's pants, poking sticks up his pantlegs. Nami bends down and growls at the child like a dog, causing him to screech in terror and delight. After a while he crawls up into Nami's lap. Jabbers some nonsense. His neck is filthy. Nami tilts his head back and closes his eyes. Breathes in the fragrance of the old house. The crack in the floor, where the snakes used to slither in when his gramma fed them a bowl of milk, has been filled in with cement. Photographs of the kolkhoz chairman and his family hang on the walls. One of them shows the chairman as a young man, leaning on a hunting rifle with his foot resting on top of something big and hairy that over the years has blurred into a grainy smudge. The radio plays some traditional folk songs with a dutar and a desperate man singing in falsetto about how he wants to ride his horse off a cliff since his lover will no longer put out for him. Nami's so tired he just wants to lay his head down on the table and sleep. The little boy bangs the table, squirming restlessly in Nami's lap. His mother admonishes him to stop and serves Nami a plate of soup.

Nami tosses the boy a little roughly off his lap and digs into the soup. It tastes good.

'So, how do you like my wife's cooking?' he hears someone say behind his back. The chairman has come home for lunch. He squints and sizes Nami up, evaluating the new muscles on his back and arms, his first white hairs, and the wrinkle between his eyebrows. He decides to opt for a jovial tone.

'Now that's what you call a cook, right?'

'My mother cooks better,' Nami snaps back. The chairman's expression hardens, but he's still uncertain how to react.

'You don't say. So you have a mother, huh?'

'Yep, imagine that. You didn't know, huh?'

'Nope,' the chairman says. 'This whole time I thought some Siberian bear shit you out of its ass.'

'There, you see? Came out all right, though, no? I've got everything I'm supposed to. Two hands, two legs ...'

The kolkhoz chairman flies up out of his seat, but Nami is ready for him and shoves the chair in his way. The chairman hits his ribs and bounces back, hissing in pain.

'I guess nobody ever told you not to reproduce, did they? Maybe that vet of yours can castrate you? Or maybe your old lady could just do you by hand?' He shoots the chairman's wife an apologetic glance.

The chairman takes a swipe at him but comes up empty, lurching to the side.

'Just stop, you don't have what it takes anymore,' Nami says wearily and sits back down to his soup. The chairman's wife stands holding her apron over her mouth. The three-handed toddler nestles against her legs. Nami eats, spoon clinking against the plate. The chairman leans on the table, breathing heavily.

'I'll make up your room,' the woman says at last, when she can no longer stand the silence. She takes the little boy by the hand and walks out.

***

Nami invites Zaza to the Sugar Cockerel candy shop, where children have been buying burnt sugar lollipops since time out of mind. A curtain of filthy rubber strips hangs in the doorway to prevent the invasion of flies, but it doesn't help too much. Zaza drinks boza, a fermented beverage made of wheat that they give to children and expectant mothers because it's high in vitamins.

'I married Alex,' Zaza says casually out of the blue.

Nami stiffens, unable to hide his shock. He slowly stirs his spoon. The tea is so black you can't even see the bottom of the cup.

'That jerk?'

'Yeah, that one.' Zaza nods with no expression.

Nami pauses. He'd like to say something quickly. The awkwardness is growing by the moment.

'Yeah, I don't know if you can imagine,' Zaza goes on, 'but it wasn't exactly easy to find a groom in my situation.'

'Sure, I know,' Nami says quickly. 'That's obvious.'

'And Alex didn't ask any questions.'

'Zaza. I don't blame you for anything,' he says. He realises he's digging his nails into the palms of his hands. Fat, red-haired Alex.

Zaza grins sarcastically. 'Well, that's nice of you.'

'So what was I supposed to do, in your opinion?'

'I don't know. Not run away?'

He lays the palm of his right hand over his face and exhales into it loudly. He can hear Zaza breathing angrily on the other side of the table. She is holding her hands on her belly, and Nami detects a slight bulge where there didn't used to be. Zaza catches his eye and grins sourly again.

'Yes, that's right. I'm expecting a baby. With that jerk.'

'Congratulations then. Eh. Seriously.'

'You don't have to pretend. Alex may be a jerk, but he loves me. He'll take care of us. And he won't abandon us.'

Nami prays in his mind that Zaza won't burst into tears. He wouldn't be able to stand it.

But she's tough. She already has that firmly clenched jaw and the two distinct wrinkles along her mouth that are typical of every strong woman he's ever met in his life. She isn't about to burst into tears that easily.

Nami orders two baklavas. He devours his immediately,

leaving not a bit of walnut stuck between his teeth. Zaza just pokes at hers.

'Eat. You have to eat for two now.'

Zaza smiles and puts a bite in her mouth. A drip of sugary syrup from the juicy baklava runs down Zaza's chin.

'You're going to have a little kid. You can sing to him and tell him the story about the Golden Horde who sleep in Kolos Mountain and will come to save us one day.' Nami smiles.

'Yes, every night.'

'So that's good. And the Spirit of the Lake. That one too.'

Zaza says nothing, chewing intently. Nami has an urge to tell her only an irresponsible madman would bring a child into the world in Boros, but instead he just encourages her to eat some more. Zaza behaves like a good little girl—like every child in Boros whose parents ever took them to the Sugar Cockerel; they had been bribed with it for so long that when they finally found themselves sitting in one of the fabled candy shop's plastic chairs, they were so overwhelmed they had no idea if the treat on their plate was worth putting in their mouth.

'I guess we can't return it, huh?' says Zaza finally as she takes the last bite.

Nami shrugs. 'Ah ... hm.'

'Well, I didn't get pregnant that time, if that's what you're asking. And I didn't catch any nasty Russian disease.'

'Hm. What I wanted to ...'

'But you ran away.'

'I'm so sorry, Zaza. I panicked ... They had rifles and they were such dumbshits.'

'I know. Later one of them shot his head off during a training exercise. Himself, can you imagine? He must've been wasted.'

'Zaza.'

'I didn't sleep a single night after it happened. I was going to jump in the well, but my Aunt Lemina saw me. They ended up locking me in a room for a couple of weeks so I couldn't hurt myself. They gave me poppy seed infusions,' she adds with a strained laugh.

'God.'

'After that, I stopped thinking about the well.'

Nami lowers his eyes.

'Where've you been?'

He breathes in as if about to say something, but then just waves his hand. 'It's a long story.'

'Ah.'

'No, really. I'll tell you someday.'

'For real?'

'For real.'

'All right then.'

'Sure.'

'So was it worth it at least?' Zaza suddenly shouts. All the guests in the candy store turn their heads to look. 'Tell me! Did you at least get anything out of going away?'

Nami sits in silence. A girl of about eight is showing off a toy of hers to the woman behind the counter: a wind-up doll. A few turns of the key and the doll in the crinoline skirt starts twirling around in circles to the theme from Swan Lake. As the motor runs out of steam, the music plays increasingly slowly and out of tune.

Nami realises that in fact he does love Zaza. In that regard nothing has changed, even if she is expecting a baby with that jerk Alex. And he's glad he's here with her.

***

'I guess this calls for shots,' the chairman says. His hand trembles as he pours the liquor, spilling a little onto the table. He hands Nami his drink, taps glasses with him, and pours a little out on the floor. 'To the memory of your gramma,' he says.

'That's right. If it wasn't for her, instead of this nice house, you'd still be living in some cowshed. To her memory!' Nami says as he throws back the shot of vodka.

'What do you want anyway? You know if I wanted to I could destroy you. One talk with the guys from the kolkhoz and tomorrow you'll be with the Spirit of the Lake.'

'Oh sure. Just like Shahnaz? That sick boy you all lynched and drowned? Is that what you'd do to me?'

The chairman stands bolt upright, eyes opening wide. For a moment it looks like he's choking. The baby starts shifting around in the cradle, bleating like a goat.

'Where is the Shahnaz family now? Where do they live?'

'Outside of Boros,' the chairman says, waving his hand toward the west. 'Where the shipyards and dry docks used to be, a little past that, there's a tumbledown house, more like a shack. His father lives there. You can tell by all the tons of crap lying all over the place.' He gives a loud belch. 'The guy's a nut.'

Nami nods toward the crib. 'Your baby's crying.'

He tosses his knapsack over his shoulder and walks out without saying goodbye. He can still hear the baby squalling as the chairman's wife comes running downstairs. She lifts the girl out of the cradle and takes her in her arms, soothing her. Then runs out onto the stoop after Nami.

'I knew your mom,' she says hurriedly.

'Really?' says Nami coolly.

'Oh, yes. We were in the same class at school. She had blue eyes. All the boys wanted her, not only Shahnaz. She was so beautiful.'

Nami feels a strong urge to hit her.

***

Instead, he punches one hand into the palm of the other. He runs down toward the port, following the road. He passes by the old filling station, then the shipyards, till he comes to the old fishing settlement, where a couple of shacks still stand. He looks behind him, and seeing Boros in the setting sun, to him in this light it looks beautiful, even including the mess in the Gypsy district and the broken-down Russian housing estate. There are pink clouds forming on the horizon. The year's first mosquitoes are starting to bite.

***

The chairman was right; one of the homes shows signs of being inhabited and is surrounded by tons of stuff. Mugs and leather belts hang from the fence, shoes single and in pairs, plastic buckets and canisters, scarves of every colour, caps, chains, ropes, tattered paper lanterns, briefcases, neoprene wetsuits and diving suits. Ranks of refrigerators and car bumpers line the fence, boat propellers, harpoons, headlights, car batteries, sinks and washbasins, beams and planks. The heaps of junk are piled so high they cover part of the windows.

A man sits on the stoop outside the house, cleaning some sort of tin container with a toothbrush. He glances up at Nami through thick prescription lenses. The man is dressed in an undershirt and track pants. His eyes are clear and bright, hair white, arms tanned and muscular.

Nami says hello and the man beckons for him to come sit beside him on the stoop. Throwing off his knapsack, Nami sits down and leans back against the peeling wall of the house. He feels like just saying hello exhausted him to the point that he can't even get another word out, so he just sits in silence.

The man continues with his work; once he's done with the tin vase, he picks up a bronze mortar, drips a few drops of lemon juice on it, and goes right on polishing. Nami closes his eyes and tests whether the sun is still hot enough to burn his skin. A moment later he wakes with a start and discovers he's fallen asleep. The man hands him a mug of tea. Nami nods his head in thanks and downs its still-hot contents in practically one gulp. The tea is strong and very sweet.

'All from the lake,' says the man with a sweep of his right hand. 'I rescued it all. The more valuable stuff I keep inside. Wedding albums. Oh, yes, you wouldn't believe it, but even photos can be saved. Letters. Wallets. Carved backgammon cases with ivory stones.'

The man smiles. It's getting dark and chilly out.

'Let's go in,' the man says, getting to his feet. Inside, he lights a kerosene lamp. Brings a piece of bread, a dish of butter, and two onions from the cupboard. Nami slowly chews his food, starting to fall asleep again. The man points to the bed and tells him to go ahead and lie down, it's the bed that belonged to his son.

The flame from the kerosene lamp casts flickering shadows over the walls of the house. Collapsing into the bed where his biological father once slept, Nami is asleep before he knows it.

***

When Nami wakes in the morning, he's having trouble breathing. For some reason he can't catch his breath. Then he realises there's a big ginger tomcat weighing down his chest. He sweeps the cat off and sits up in bed. Then it dawns on him where he is. He can smell the mustiness of the old home and the indistinct odour of metal and petroleum jelly. The man sits at the table, reading aloud. He has on a worn but clean shirt and black pants.

*The land of Zebulun and the land of Naphtali,*
*Toward the sea, beyond the Jordan,*
*Galilee of the Gentiles,*
*The people that sat in darkness*
*Saw a great light,*
*And to them that sat in the region and shadow of death,*
*To them did light spring up.*

'Gospel of Matthew,' the man says cheerfully in Nami's direction. Nami gets up and stretches. It's still sinking in where he actually is. The man looks at him calmly, no questions, no annoyance.

'I was sent here by the chairman of the kolkhoz, who lives in our house now,' Nami says. The words coming out of him feel as though they're wrapped in sheathing; they aren't connected to him, they don't belong to him. 'My mom is Marie Anna. That means I'm your grandson.'

The man takes off his glasses and cleans them on his shirt.

'That's a misunderstanding,' he says. 'I have no grandson. I don't even have a son. I have no wife or any other relatives. My only friend is the Lord Jesus Christ.'

Nami shrugs. Punches his fist into his open hand a few times and walks out in front of the house. The sun is already out, but the shadows are still long and the air chilly. Why should he be surprised that he's run into a madman at the end of his journey? It couldn't have been any other way.

The man comes out behind Nami and sits on the stoop. The ginger cat trails behind him, jumping into his lap. The man buries his hand in the tomcat's long fur and pets him gently.

'You're not my grandson,' he says amicably. 'I had one son, and he died pure as an angel. Your mother was anything but a virgin when it happened.'

Nami stares off silently into the distance. He can only make out the water from the reflection of the pale morning sun.

'The girl probably had a close call. I don't blame her for making up that story. God knows what led her to do what she did—or how any of us would have behaved in a similar situation. She was probably in trouble and didn't know where to go. Let him who is without guilt throw the first stone.'

Nami grasps hold of the railing and suddenly realises his legs are shaking, as though he were sick.

'Shahnaz was a good boy. And what a brain he had! Was even faster than the teacher when it came to arithmetic. And tidy too. Always made sure everything in my workshop was neatly arranged, according to size. I had everything all lined up—hammers, screws, even a ball of thread—everything in alignment, not so much as a pushpin sticking out of line.' The man smiles faintly. 'His mother used to sing to him when she put him to sleep, from the time he was little up until he was seventeen. She always had to sing the same three songs before he'd fall asleep. Every so often he'd throw a tantrum, and he never got along with the other kids, but he never hurt anyone. Nobody. And he called me *dodda*.' He pauses a moment before going on. 'They came by here one evening. It was January, sun going down, about seven o'clock. The kolkhoz chairman was the leader, but they were all here—the shaman, your grandfather, all the big shots and their old ladies—and everyone was yelling, 'Give us that little bastard!' None of us knew what was going on, but soon the whole house was full of em. They dragged Shahnaz out of bed, poor boy was terrified, screaming and crying. You can imagine. Ach, good God,' the man says calmly, still stroking the cat. 'My wife started yelling, threw herself at them, tearing off her clothes. But she couldn't make them stop. The shaman was shaking his rattle, saying a great evil had taken place and it had to be undone. Shahnaz was crying out, *Dodda, dodda,* but I couldn't do a thing. I saw them carry him out to the yard, and they jumped up and down on him and they were kicking him. Then they tied him up to a jeep and set it on fire. If you'd heard him scream! There's not a day that goes by that I don't hear his screams. Not a day I don't pray to my dear God to spare me from those screams. Then they drove him like that to the lake. The boy was probably already dead when they threw him in, I pray he was.'

The man says it as calmly as if he were talking about the bus schedule. The cat on his lap stretches and jumps down to the stoop. From there, it heads out along the wall on the hunt or perhaps in search of romantic adventure. The man picks up a nut without looking, then grabs a rag and mindlessly starts cleaning the grease off it.

'I wasn't able to tell him goodbye. He left this world so innocent and young! It was a great sin, boy. I pray for all those sinners, that the Lord have mercy on them. But it was a terrible sin. My hair turned white that night. My wife went out of her mind, and a week later she went down and followed her son into the lake. Now I'm here by myself,' the man says, awkwardly throwing up his hands. The brass nut jumps from his lap to the ground. Nami bends down to pick it up and hands it back to the man, who just stares ahead absently.

'Suddenly all my strength drained away after it happened. Like a tidal wave had swept over me, I lost all my strength. I fell down on the ground and couldn't get up.'

He pauses again for a moment.

'You notice there's nothing around to hear anymore? Used to be a fighter plane would swoop through every now and then—Russkies trying to keep us spooked. Remember all those parades? Talk about a racket! You could hear the ships in port honking all the way up here. Fish plant blowing the end of the shifts. Camels grumbling, donkeys braying. Public broadcast system, now that was fun ... speakers all over the streets playing those socialist songs! Now the place is so quiet, it's like everything is dead and gone.'

'It's nice to me,' Nami says. He crumples a blade of grass in his hand.

'Years ago, Russian divers went down looking for a drowned submarine. I used to go and watch em and that gave me an idea. For a couple bottles of vodka they taught me how to dive and left me their diving suits and gear. My idea was I would go down in the lake and find Shahnaz and bring him back home. If I keep diving long enough, I'll meet him again, I'm sure. The Lake Spirit doesn't like it when people end up down there at the wrong time for the wrong reasons. He'll want to give him back, I know it.'

'But it's been eighteen years!'

'As long as my body serves me I'll keep looking for my son.'

'That's insane.'

'I know he's long dead. I just don't want him down there underwater alone. I want him to know that I'm looking for him.'

'So that's how you find all these things.'

'That's right. When I dig around in the mud, it stirs up and you can't see a thing. But when I do find something, something personal, it's always worth it. Chess set with an inlaid board. Some bits of a brocade slipper. A comb inlaid with mother-of-pearl. Somebody's school notebook cover.

When there's a name on it I know, I return it to the original owners. Gave a doll back to a girl who's ten years older now than when she lost it. She thanked me like I'd brought her the golden fleece. Sometimes I find trinkets and stuff that belonged to people who aren't alive anymore. So I give it to the survivors. Some of them cry they're so moved. Others toss the damn thing the second I'm out the gate.'

'How about a body? Have you ever found one of those?'

The man shrugs. 'Not yet. But I've found fish unlike any I ever saw before in my life. A five-metre-long beluga. Tiny fluorescent gobies. Truly a joy to behold. But that's a long time ago now.'

The red-haired cat rubs against Nami's pantleg, and he gently nudges him away with his foot.

'Let's eat,' the man says.

'Why are you taking care of me?'

The man turns to him with an uncomprehending look. 'Why? Because you need it, son. Besides, it's just bread and onions,' he shrugs.

So then who really is his father, Nami wonders out loud. The man answers to the effect that some doors are better left unopened, but Nami snaps back that he can spare him the clichés. He's a grown-up and wants to know whose blood runs through his veins.

'I don't know. Shahnaz was crazy about your mother and he dogged her every step. She was beautiful the way only seventeen-year-old girls from Boros can be. He knew she was having secret rendezvous with some Russian soldier. Someone from the Russian garrison.'

'Russian garrison?'

'Son, I don't know. That's what Shahnaz wrote in his diary. He said he followed them when they went to meet in the woods. It lasted a long time. He was sad about it the way only a boy in love can be.'

'No.'

'Look, I understand. Just forget it.'

'No, no!'

Nami takes a running start and slams his head into the man's chest, shoving him up against the wall. Gasping for breath, the older man puts Nami in a headlock and holds him there a while. As soon as he sees that Nami is no longer fighting, he wraps him in a hug and the two of them stay that way, hugging, half a minute, a minute. Then the man says he'll make eggs.

***

He makes the eggs scrambled and fries bread to go with them. The two of them eat in silence on the stoop. Then the man tells Nami to wash the dishes and starts packing his wetsuit to go. Nami sits a long time not moving, just staring at the lake. Then he says he'd like to go too. He'd like to learn how to dive so he can look for Shahnaz and all of those things that people lost with him. And so he can finally see the fucking Spirit for himself. The man points to a wetsuit hanging on the pole for drying comforters.

Nami rests his hands on his belly; it's nice being well fed again for a change. But no matter how deep down he reaches, he can't find the slightest scrap of feeling inside of him. There's just a long, empty burrow that some wild animal dug in there once upon a time. He's left fragments of himself behind in all the people he's loved, and now there is nothing for him.

'I know for a fact there's no Spirit there,' Nami says casually as he takes off his shoe and pours out the sand. The man glances up at him coolly, kicking his moped off its stand.

'Let's go,' he says patiently. 'Get on.'

'There's definitely no fucking Spirit here. Maybe there was before, maybe. But now all there is in that sewer is a bunch of toxins and corpses and junk.'

'Are you done with the bullshit? Because I'm going,' the man says, starting the bike.

***

They ride the moped almost all the way down to the tide line. Then change into the wetsuits and walk together wordlessly over the dry, cracked, salty bottom till they reach the water's edge. A faint breeze pushes tiny spiked balls of fluff carrying the seeds of some desert plant across the hardened shore, but Nami can't hear their quiet scratching with the neoprene hood over his head. He doesn't smell the stench of the water with the respirator on over his face. The water is icy, but Nami doesn't feel it through the neoprene.

The lake slowly opens up and Nami enters into it.

## Acknowledgments

Thanks belong to my dear private reviewers, Veronika Siska and Anna Zonová; to Honza Němec for being my second authorial self and for making editing with him so easy. To Adrian, for his unwavering support.

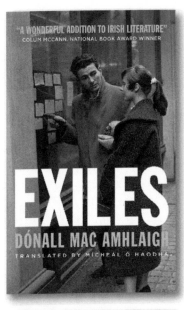

# LA BLANCHE

Maï-Do Hamisultane

Translated from French
by Suzy Ceulan Hughes

£8.99
978-1-912681-23-5

# THE NIGHT CIRCUS AND OTHER STORIES

Uršuľa Kovalyk

Translated from Slovak
by Julia and Peter Sherwood

£8.99
978-1-912681-04-4

# A GLASS EYE

Miren Agur Meabe

Translated from Basque
by Amaia Gabantxo

£8.99
978-1-912109-54-8

# PARTHIAN TRANSLATIONS

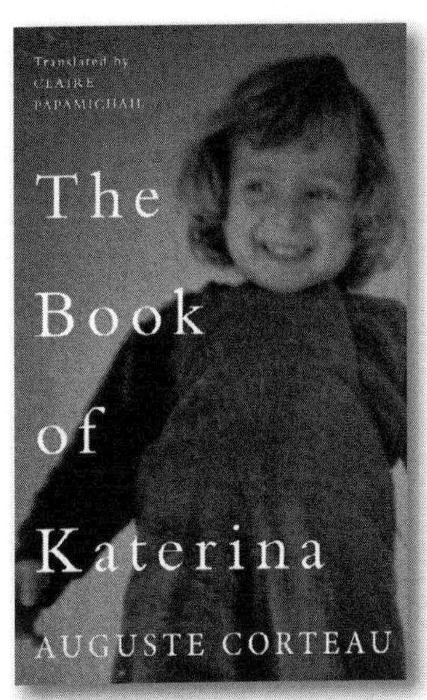


## THE BOOK OF KATERINA

Auguste Corteau

Translated from Greek
by Claire Papamichail

**Out 2021**

£10.00
978-1-912681-26-6

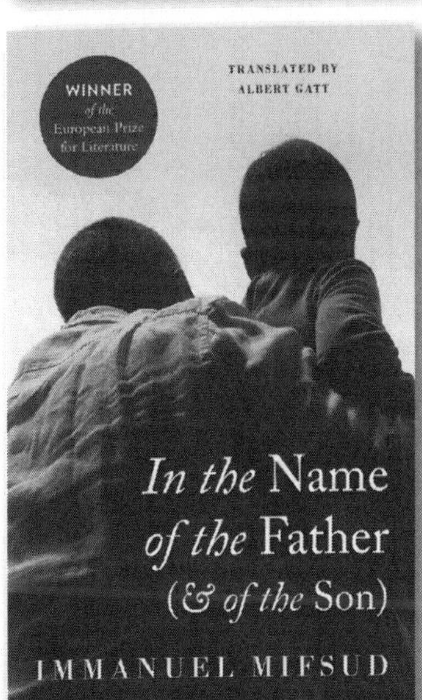


## IN THE NAME OF THE FATHER (& OF THE SON)

Immanuel Mifsud

Translated from Maltese
by Albert Gatt

£6.99
978-1-912681-30-3

# HER MOTHER'S HANDS

Karmele Jaio

Translated from Basque
by Kristin Addis

£8.99
978-1-912109-55-5

# WOMEN WHO BLOW ON KNOTS

Ece Temelkuran

Translated from Turkish
by Alexander Dawe

£9.99
978-1-910901-69-4

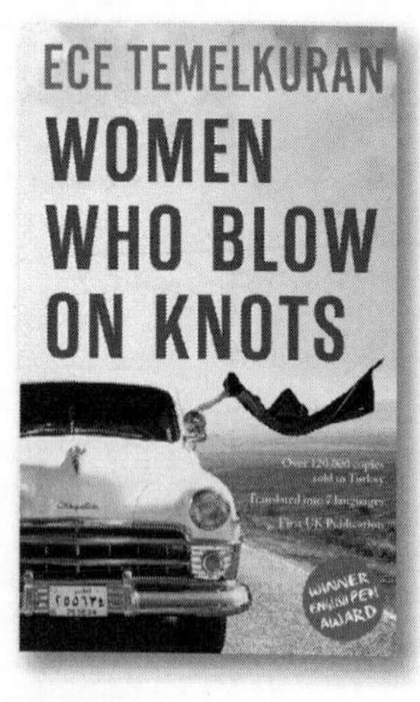

# THE HOUSE OF THE DEAF MAN

Peter Krištúfek

Translated from Slovak
by Julia and Peter Sherwood

£11.99
978-1-909844-27-8